PRAISE FOR
THE THINGS SHE'S SEEN

"Packs a massive punch." —*Locus*

★ "An #ownvoices story that empowers its female heroines, giving them pride in their lineage and power in remembering." —*Kirkus Reviews*, starred review

"A fusion of ghost story and crime thriller." —*The Saturday Paper*

"The two Australian Aboriginal girls at the center of *The Things She's Seen* discover just how poisonous silencing can be and how much power it takes to finally break through it." —*The Bulletin*

"An intense, addictive book." —*Readings*

"A ghost story as well as a psychological thriller, *The Things She's Seen* seamlessly weaves together the poetic and the everyday. A magnificent and life-giving novel." —Justine Larbalestier, author of *My Sister Rosa*

"Fascinating, gripping, innovative." —*Magpies* Magazine

"Terrible crimes lie at the center of this story; viewed through the eyes of young women of unquenchable spirit, they can be approached, examined, and ultimately solved. This novel will turn gazes in the right direction, and make the caw of every crow more resonant." —Margo Lanagan, Printz Honor winner for *Tender Morsels*

THE
THINGS
SHE'S
SEEN

THE THINGS SHE'S SEEN

AMBELIN AND EZEKIEL KWAYMULLINA

EMBER

Text copyright © 2018 by Ambelin Kwaymullina and Ezekiel Kwaymullina
Cover art copyright © 2021 by Stephen Carroll/Trevillion Images

Visit us on the Web! GetUnderlined.com

Educators and librarians, for a variety of teaching tools, visit us at RHTeachersLibrarians.com

Library of Congress Cataloging-in-Publication Data is available upon request.
ISBN 978-1-9848-4878-9 (trade) — ISBN 978-1-9848-4937-3 (lib. bdg.) — ISBN 978-1-9848-4938-0 (ebook)

Printed in the United States of America
10 9 8 7 6 5 4 3 2 1
First Ember Edition 2021

ISBN 978-1-9848-4953-3 (pbk.)

THE
THINGS
SHE'S
SEEN

Beth

THE TOWN

My dad looked like crap.

His blond hair was flat and grubby, and his skin seemed too big for his bones. The muscly, tanned guy who'd built me a two-story tree house when I was a kid had been replaced by a pale shell of a man who didn't build anything.

You'd think it would be me who looked different. Dad said I didn't. I couldn't tell, since I didn't cast a reflection anymore. But if I looked the same, then the face smiling out from the pictures on the walls of our house must still be my face: curly dark hair, round cheeks, brown skin like Mum's, and blue eyes like Dad's. Only I didn't smile as much now. Dad barely smiled at all.

He pressed his hand to his chest, out of breath from climbing up this rocky hill. There were a bunch of rock formations like this one around here, rising up from a flat red plain that was dotted with trees. I liked the trees. They were old and white and twisty, spiraling upward to fling out their leaves as if they were hoping to touch the sky. I liked the sky too; there seemed to be more of it here than in the city. There were no buildings to block it out. No big ones, anyway. We could see much of the town from where we stood: a sprawl of houses surrounded by the scattered trees, with a long river to the north. The town was covered in the same dust that coated everything, including our car and my dad's rumpled shirt and pants. The dust hadn't touched my clothes, of course. My dress would always be as yellow and crisp as it had been on the day Aunty Viv drove me to the birthday party.

Dad took a step closer to the edge of the hill, gazing outward.

"I don't think you're going to solve the case from up here," I told him.

His gaze shifted in my direction. His eyes were bright with tears. Sometimes he couldn't even look at me without sobbing. Today the tears didn't fall. But I could hear them in his voice when he said, "I miss you, Beth."

"I'm right here, Dad."

Except we both knew I wasn't. At least, not in the way he wanted me to be.

The accident had happened so fast. One minute I'd been sitting in Aunty Viv's sedan, everything normal. Then I'd heard the four-wheel drive plowing through the bushes as it tore down the embankment. I'd looked up to see it hurtling at me, and . . . nothing.

I didn't remember the actual dying part.

In fact, I *felt* as if I was still a living, breathing girl. Right now, for instance, I could see the town, hear the wind, smell the eucalyptus from the trees, and taste the gritty dust. I just couldn't touch any of it.

This wasn't how I'd imagined being dead, not that I'd ever spent much time thinking about it. But Mum had died when I was just a baby, and her two sisters—Aunty Viv and Aunty June—had always told me I'd see her again. Aunty June reckoned that Mum was "on another side." Her husky voice echoed through my memory: *This world's got a lot of sides, like those crystals your Aunty Viv hangs in her window, and your mum's just on a different side to us.* So I'd always figured that when *I* passed over to another side, Mum would be there to meet me.

She hadn't been. But I sometimes had a sense that she was waiting somewhere ahead—I'd be seeing her, I knew it. What I didn't know was exactly when. The *when* didn't matter so much, though, since I didn't count minutes or hours anymore. Days began when the sun rose and ended when it set. In between, the connections I made—like the ways I helped my dad, or didn't help him—were what told me if I was moving forward or backward. As my Grandpa Jim had once said to me, *Life doesn't move through time, Bethie. Time moves through life.*

Dad was staring at me with the lost expression I'd come to hate. I waved encouragingly at the town. "Why don't you go investigate?"

He stared for a moment longer. Then he turned away and wiped at his eyes, focusing his attention on the houses below us.

"I *am* investigating. I'm getting a sense of the place." His voice was raspy. He drew in a deep breath, and added in a more even tone, "It reminds me of where your mum and I

5

grew up." His mouth twisted as if he'd tasted something bad. "Local police officers can have a lot of power in a place like this."

He was thinking about his father. My grandpa on Dad's side—who I'd never actually met—had been a cop for thirty years, and he wasn't a good guy. Dad said his old man thought the law was there to protect some people and punish others. And Aboriginal people were the "others." Grandpa and Grandma Teller had thrown Dad out when he started seeing Mum, and they'd never wanted anything to do with me, their Aboriginal granddaughter.

"Do you think there are police like your dad in this town?" I asked.

"Maybe. Maybe not. Places like this are changing. Places everywhere are changing. Slowly, but it's happening." He sighed and shook his head. "I'm just not sure there's anything here to investigate."

I didn't like the sound of that. I needed Dad to be interested in this case. My father was stuck in grief like a man caught in a muddy swamp. I had to get him to walk forward until he'd left the mire behind. Otherwise he'd just keep sinking until the water swallowed him.

"Someone *did* die in that fire," I pointed out.

That was why Dad was here, because an inferno had engulfed a children's home and killed . . . well, somebody. The body had been burned too badly to identify, so the cops were working on getting DNA or dental records to find out who it was. But at least it wasn't one of the kids. They'd all escaped, which I was glad about; the littlest was only ten, same age as my cousin Sophie.

"You can't give up on this case before you even know who's dead," I told him.

"The only people living in that place besides the kids were the home's director and the nurse. So it's likely one of them," Dad replied. "Probably the nurse, because he was tall, and so is our corpse."

"Then what happened to the director?" I demanded. "There were no other bodies, so he can't be dead. Which means he's vanished. *Very* mysteriously."

"The local police might have found him in the time it took us to drive here," Dad said. "Don't go overcomplicating this, Beth. The fire was likely accidental, remember."

"You don't know that for certain! The faulty wiring is only a . . . What did they call it? 'Preliminary assessment'?"

Dad snorted. "Preliminary or not, the local cops could've handled all of this. At least until there was more information." He gave a frustrated shake of his head. "I've only been sent here because of Oversight."

Oversight was the name of an initiative the government had introduced after a series of bungled murder investigations. Whenever there was a possible homicide, an experienced senior detective had to look things over to make sure it was all being done right. Dad had lots to say about how the money put into Oversight should've been spent on more resources and better training instead.

Except Oversight wasn't really why he was here. Dad's

boss, Rachel, thought Dad was still grieving and not ready for anything too difficult yet. I knew because I'd followed Dad around the police station and listened to what people were saying after he'd left a room. Rachel had figured she was doing him a favor by giving him an easy assignment. She was wrong. My father needed a real mystery. Something to solve. Something to do.

I was trying to think of another way to interest Dad in the case when his phone rang. He took it out of his pocket and cast a quick glance down at the screen. Then he put it away, letting it ring out into silence.

I didn't need to ask who was calling. It had to be one of Mum's brothers or sisters. The Uncles and the Aunties had been taking care of my father since the accident. Dad hadn't minded so much about Aunty June, Uncle Mick, and Uncle Kelvin constantly checking in on him, but lately they'd been trying to get him to make up with Aunty Viv, which he did mind.

"The crash wasn't Aunty Viv's fault," I told him. "It was the other driver who lost control of his car, and it wasn't his fault either. There was nothing more to it than rain and a sharp turn on a slippery road—the guy wasn't even speeding! It was an *accident*, Dad."

No reaction.

"You're not being fair to Aunty Viv."

Still nothing. But deep down inside, he must know he was being unfair. He just couldn't stop himself from blaming her, which made no sense. It wasn't like she'd *wanted* to get out of the crash with nothing more than a concussion and a few bruises. She'd come round to the house once, to pound on the front door and scream, "You think I don't wish it was me who was dead? You know how I loved that girl!"

Dad hadn't opened the door, and after a few minutes she'd slumped down on the step.

I'd gotten so busy taking care of Dad that I hadn't looked in on Aunty Viv as often as I should have, and I'd been shocked at the sight of her. For starters, she was wearing an old gray tracksuit. Aunty Viv hated gray, and she never wore tracksuits—it was Aunty June who had the wardrobe full of gym clothes and the cupboard full of health bars. Aunty Viv ate chocolate biscuits and said a few extra kilos just meant there was more of her to love.

As if the tracksuit wasn't bad enough, Aunty Viv's feet were encased in flat sandals, showing unpainted toenails. I hadn't even known she owned any sensible shoes, and I'd never seen her nails without sparkles. She'd looked nothing like my round, bubbly Aunty who made every space brighter just by being in it.

I'd tried speaking to her, even though I'd known by then that only Dad could see and hear me.

"I don't want you to be the one who died, Aunty. What would your kids do without you? Ella's so little! And Sophie and Charlie need you too. Especially Charlie—who's going to keep him out of trouble if you're not around?"

I'd had no impact, of course. She'd just kept on sitting. After a while, tears had started to roll down her brown cheeks and she'd sunk her head in her hands. Her grief had reminded me so much of Dad's that I'd panicked and yelled, "You have to be okay! *I can't be the reason anyone else falls apart!*"

A few moments later, Aunty had stopped crying. When she raised her head, there was a slight frown on her face, as if she'd been struck by a realization. The frown had faded into bewilderment as she gazed down at her tracksuited body— she clearly couldn't recognize herself in what she was wearing any more than I had.

She'd stood up and called to Dad, "I'm always here if you need me, Michael." Then she'd walked off with her shoulders a little straighter than they'd been before. I liked to think that her spirit heard mine, even though her ears didn't.

When I next checked on her, she was wearing her favorite pink dress. The toenails still weren't done, and her shoes still had no heels, but I knew she was going to be okay.

I wanted Dad to be okay too. And I wanted him to speak to Aunty Viv.

I tried again. "She lost me as well, you know. All the family did. More than you, even, because they can't see me."

Something roared to life in Dad's eyes. "*No one* lost you more." He turned and stormed back down the hill.

Stupid thing to say, Beth. And he was right; he had lost me the most. Not because he loved me the most, but because he couldn't remember me the way the rest of my family could.

When the others spoke of me, they talked about what I'd loved and what I'd hated and what had made me laugh. They talked about me even when they were desperately sad about my death—in fact, *especially* when they were desperately sad. Their memory of me had become the glue that held everyone together, and I loved them for that. It was as if I, Beth Teller, was holding my family up, and so everything great they went on to do would be a little bit because of me, and a little bit like I was doing it as well.

Dad was different. He and I were the reverse of each other: I couldn't remember my death; Dad couldn't remember my life—at least, not without focusing on how it ended. I was sure it was the reason only he could see me. No one but him needed reminding that I'd been so much more than a few screeching moments of chaos and wreckage. That I was *still* so much more.

Except now he was stomping away.

On the other hand, at least he wasn't crying.

I thought about that. No tears was surely a good thing. *In fact* . . .

I grinned. Maybe I could add "make Dad angry" to the list of things I was doing to keep him headed in the right direction.

Pleased, I trailed after my father.

THE HOME

What had once been the children's home was now a pile of blackened timber.

We were well out of town, surrounded by trees that scattered across the red earth and crowded together along the edge of the river in the distance. This whole area must have been swarming with police right after the fire. But now forensics and arson had been and gone, and the burned body taken for an autopsy. There was only the rubble and the quiet and the lingering tang of smoke in the air.

A crow flapped down to perch on a splintered beam jabbing upward from the ruin of the home. I waved. Sometimes it seemed as if animals could sense that I was about. The crow fluffed out its feathers, tilting its head to one side. Almost as if it was asking me a question. Then it flew off. Maybe it *had* seen me and thought I was shooing it away? Or maybe the crow had always been going to take off right then. My science teacher said that just because two things happened together didn't mean one was because of the other, or as she put it: *Correlation does not imply causation.*

But Dad said that was scientist talk, not police talk, and if two things happened together, you'd suspect the first thing had caused the second until it could provide you with an alibi.

He was pacing around the ruin with the case file tucked under his arm. He'd got over being mad sometime during the drive between the hill and the home. I knew he wasn't really angry with me anyway. More like angry *about* me, or at least about me dying. I could understand that. I'd been mad after the accident too. I wasn't supposed to be dead before I even made it to my sixteenth birthday. In fact, when I let myself think too much about the unfairness of it all, I still got mad now. But I couldn't lose myself to that, not when Dad had been left behind twice over. He'd told me once that when Mum died, it had been looking after me that had kept him going. Now what was keeping him going was *me* looking after *him*.

I wished Mum was here to help. Aunty June always said nobody had ever been sad around my mum because she radiated happiness like a fire radiated heat. But it was just me here, and Dad, and I didn't like the frustrated expression on his face. He wasn't seeing anything interesting in that ruin.

I asked the first question I could think of. "Why did they build the home so far from the town—especially when it was supposed to help kids who'd been in trouble? Doesn't seem like there's much for them to do out here."

"The idea was to get them back to nature, make them self-sufficient. They were supposed to learn to cook their

13

own meals, clean up after themselves, that sort of thing," he replied. "Besides, it wasn't purpose-built as a children's home. Originally it was just a big old house, belonging to a local family."

He reached into his file and pulled out a photo, holding it up in front of the ruin. "This was taken a few weeks ago."

I hadn't seen the photo before. Dad hadn't wanted me looking in the case file, because it contained pictures of the body. But this photo was of a house. I walked over to him, peering at the image of a sprawling white weatherboard with wide verandas. A group of about ten kids stood out front, alongside three adults. The kids were all different ages and different colors—black kids, white kids, brown kids. None of them were smiling, or at least not properly. The corners of their mouths were turned up, but the smiles didn't reach their eyes. I guessed I wouldn't feel like smiling properly either if I was stuck in a home for kids "in trouble," whatever that meant. They'd all been rushed off to the city by child services after the fire. I hoped they'd been sent somewhere they liked better than this place.

I pointed to one of the tall adults in the photo, a lean, pale guy wearing glasses. "Is that the nurse?"

Dad shook his head. "No. That's Alexander Sholt. He's the one who set up the foundation that funds the home. He donated the house as well; it was his family who used to own it."

"He donated a whole *house*? Guess he must be rich."

"Yes, I believe that he is." He gestured to the other two

adults. "That's the nurse, Martin Flint. And beside him is the director, Tom Cavanagh."

The nurse was tall and clean-shaven, with brown hair that stuck out in all directions. The director was short and stocky and had a bushy black beard. They were both beaming proudly.

"It looks as if they liked their jobs," I said. "What exactly *were* their jobs, anyway?"

"Nurse Flint took care of the kids' nutrition, first aid, and general health and well-being. Director Cavanagh managed the home, and ran classes—English and math and the like." He sighed. "Neither of them were from around these parts. They both came here to try to help these kids."

There was a note of sadness in his voice, and I knew he was thinking about how Nurse Flint had died here.

You can't bring him back, Dad. But you can find out what happened to him.

I almost said it out loud. But I didn't need to. Dad dropped the photo back into the file and returned his attention to the ruin. Then he started speaking, only more to himself than to me, going over what had happened: "Fire starts around ten p.m. Alarm goes off, and the kids follow the fire drill like they're supposed to, and make it to safety."

"Except they said they were out of the home before the alarm went off," I pointed out. "But that can't be right, can it? The wind couldn't have told them to run, like they said."

"Not the wind," Dad agreed. "But the kids might have made up a story instead of owning up to breaking a rule. So, one of them could have been up past bedtime, seen the fire start, and warned the others. We should know more when the psychologists get through talking to them. Not that any of them are saying much right now."

"Do you think they're hiding something?"

"I think kids who've been in trouble don't like speaking to people in authority about anything. So it's no surprise they're not talking. If any of them do remember something relevant, someone will call me."

He glanced around the clearing and shook his head.

"Those kids were from the city. Taking them a long way from home, where there's nothing much for them to do except learn to be 'responsible'—I can't see that it was the best way to help them. Seems like this place was run on some old-fashioned ideas. Child services is going to sort something new out for them now."

He lapsed into silence again. I prodded him with words. "Why didn't Nurse Flint get out in time, if the alarm went off?"

He shrugged. "Something slowed him down. He was overcome by smoke, maybe. Or . . ."

"Or what?"

"I suppose it's possible that he was dead before the fire began. Or unconscious."

I hadn't thought of that! "You think the director killed him? Or hurt him? Maybe there was a fight, and the nurse got knocked out!"

Dad shook his head. "It's unlikely there was a fistfight and an unrelated problem with the wiring in the space of a few

16

hours. It's far more likely Flint died *because* of the fire, and that the director's missing for the same reason—he probably panicked in the flames and the smoke and ran out into the night. There's a lot of land out here, and not many people. If he took a wrong turn, away from the town, he could be well lost."

"Then why haven't they found him? They found that girl who was wandering around out here, and she wasn't even from the home."

"True, but she wasn't difficult to find—she was just meandering along by the river."

"We should go talk to her. She might have seen Cavanagh, be able to tell us which way he was headed. Or she might have seen something else useful."

Dad grunted.

I persisted. "I know she didn't remember much when they first interviewed her, but she might now. Don't you say that sometimes people don't realize they've seen something important until later?"

"She's not likely to be very reliable, Beth. She was, um, that is . . ."

He thought I was still a baby. "She was high."

He cast a startled glance at me. I rolled my eyes. "I was listening when your boss first told you about the case. And it's not like I don't know drugs exist."

"Ah. Yes. Well." He tugged at his collar. "Beth, you never . . . that is, you didn't—"

"No, Dad, I never did drugs." I gazed down at the ground. "At least, not *many* . . ."

He spluttered. I looked up at him and grinned. "Kidding, Dad."

"That's not funny."

But I started laughing and so did he, and for a second, we could have been any father and daughter. Until Dad's laughter stopped, choking off into a gasp that was close to a sob.

He'd forgotten I was dead. Until he hadn't.

Dad opened his mouth to speak and I knew he was going to tell me he missed me again. I didn't want to hear it. Why couldn't he be like Aunty June?

There'd been a day, not that long after I'd died, when Aunty June had been babysitting my many cousins. They'd been sad about me, so Aunty June had told them about the time I'd made Aunty Viv a birthday cake and accidentally used salt instead of sugar. Aunty Viv had said it was the best cake ever. She'd almost made it through an entire slice before throwing up.

The cousins thought that was hilarious, especially Aunty Viv's kids. Sophie had giggled about it for an entire day. And Aunty June had said to them all: *Just because our girl's on another side doesn't mean we have to stop loving her or that she's stopped loving us. And it's okay to be sad, but you can't love someone only with tears. There's got to be laughter too.*

I strode toward the car, pretending that I hadn't noticed Dad choke up. Pretending that nothing was wrong. "C'mon, Dad. Let's go talk to that witness!"

I wasn't sure he'd follow me.

But he did.

THE WITNESS

The witness had been taken to the local hospital for a general checkup, and to have the drugs flushed out of her system.

The only hospital I'd ever been to before was the towering building where Uncle Mick had gone after his heart attack. The entire family had camped out at that place while we were waiting for news. A stuck-up doctor had asked if we needed *quite* so many family members there, and Aunty June had yelled at him, which had almost got us kicked out. But then Aunty Viv had burst into tears, and the littlest cousins— never ones to miss a cue—had started crying too. Since no one had wanted to evict tiny, sobbing children, they'd left us alone. Then we'd got the word that Uncle Mick was going to be okay, and Dad had bought us all chocolates and chips from the vending machine to celebrate.

But the hospital in this town looked nothing like the one in the city that Uncle Mick had been in. It was a jumbled weatherboard building that sprawled out in all directions, as if additions had just been tacked on wherever was most convenient as the years went by. The exterior was painted a cheery bright blue, and crows perched on the rooftop, lining the big sign that said HOSPITAL.

Dad and I walked into a waiting area filled with people. A *loud* waiting area. Everyone was chatting—sharing news, asking about each other's families and kids. Talking about the fire too. I tilted my head to one side, listening to the hub-bub of conversation.

"It's so terrible, that poor man dying . . ."

"Thank heaven the children are safe . . ."

"I hope they find Tom Cavanagh soon . . ."

"My Rosie's helping with the search. Says they haven't found a trace of him yet . . ."

"They say it was bad wiring. I said to Jim, 'We must get our electrics checked . . .'"

I stopped listening. They didn't know any more than I did, and no one here was overcome with grief or anxiety, which meant no one had been close to Tom Cavanagh or Martin Flint.

Dad strode toward the nurses' station in the far corner, which was surrounded by a small but determined group of people complaining about how long it was taking to see the doctor. One of the nurses—a blond, harassed-looking woman—came hurrying over to intercept Dad.

"I'm so sorry," she said, "but one of our doctors is off with the flu. It's put us terribly behind. Is there any chance you could come back tomorrow?"

Dad held up his identification. "I'm a detective. I need

to interview the witness to the fire at the children's home. I understand she's being treated here?"

The nurse's tired blue eyes lit up in relief as she realized Dad wasn't another patient. "Oh, yes!" She pointed to a hallway that led off the waiting area. "The wards are just through there. I'll show y—"

She broke off as a gust of wind slammed the front door open and sent a cloud of dust whirling into the room. Dad shoved the door shut, but people were already coughing, and some of the older ones didn't sound so good.

The nurse heaved a sigh. "Um, can you see yourself through? We'll be right here if you need anything."

"I'll be fine on my own," Dad reassured her.

I walked ahead of him into the hallway. It was lined with doors set with small panes of glass, and I peered through the nearest one into a long room filled with rows of beds. Most of the beds were occupied by people Dad's age or older, but one held a thin, dark-haired girl.

I called over my shoulder to Dad, "I think she's in—"

That was as far as I got before a voice spoke over mine. "You police? You here about that fire?"

There was another girl, standing in a doorway farther down the hall. She had short black hair and pale skin, and was wearing a hospital gown with a long green jumper over it. If this was the witness, then they'd succeeded in getting the drugs out of her system, because her gaze was focused. In fact, everything about her was sharp, from her angled cheekbones to the spikiness of her hair and the glint in her dark eyes.

21

Dad stepped past me to smile at the girl. "Yes, I'm a detective here about the fire. Are you the one who was out there that night?"

"That's me."

"I'd like to speak to you about what you saw, if you feel up to it."

She looked him up and down, and sniffed like she wasn't impressed. Then she nodded and vanished into the room behind her. Dad followed.

This room looked exactly like the other ward room, except it contained only a single patient. Our witness was sitting on a bed with her legs stretched out and her head turned away from us so she could stare out the window. There wasn't that much to see out there—just leaves and dust swirling in the afternoon light—but she seemed fascinated by the view. Or maybe she was just ignoring us. Well, ignoring Dad. Everyone ignored me, the invisible girl.

Dad pulled up a chair and sat by the bed. I positioned myself at his shoulder.

"My name is Michael," he said to the girl. "Would you mind telling me your name?"

She answered, without looking at him, "Shouldn't you already know that, *Detective*?"

I sighed. "I guess she doesn't remember she wasn't with it enough to tell anyone her name when they found her."

The witness didn't hear me, of course. But after a moment, she turned toward Dad and said, "I'm Isobel Catching. *You* can call me Catching."

Dad raised an eyebrow. "*Catching?* That's an unusual last name."

She shrugged. "My Great-Great-Grandma was good at catching stray cattle, so the white boss called her Catching. Wasn't like she could say no, back then."

Dad blinked. "You're Aboriginal?"

Her lip curled. "What, you think I'm not brown enough? You think all Aboriginal people are the same color?"

"No. I don't think that," Dad answered. "Sorry for the misunderstanding. Matter of fact, my wife was Aboriginal."

She opened her eyes very wide and spoke in a tone dripping with sarcasm: "Wow, really? Then I guess you and I are going to be best friends."

I frowned at Catching. There was no need for her to be mean! But Dad didn't seem to mind. He just kept talking in that same gentle voice: "Catching, can you tell me about anything you saw the night of the fire?"

She slouched against the pillows. "Maybe I didn't see anything. Or maybe I did. Depends."

"Depends on what?"

She looked at me—or, no, she didn't, she looked into the space I was standing in for a second, then away again. "On if you'll believe me."

"I'm here to listen to anything you have to say," Dad promised.

"Yeah, you say that *now*. But when I start talking, you're gonna tell me there's no such thing as monsters and other-places."

Monsters? Other-places? "I think she's messing with you, Dad."

He gave the faintest shake of his head. He didn't think so, and when I returned my attention to Catching, I saw why. Her gaze had shifted inward, and the mocking glint had vanished from her eyes. She was staring at something only she could see. Whatever it was made her nostrils flare and her lips press together. I didn't know what could scare this fearless girl, but whatever it was, it was no joke and no trick.

"I can believe in monsters and, um, other-places," Dad said.

Catching hunched her shoulders. "It'll take too long. This thing didn't even start with the fire."

I realized she *wanted* to talk. She just needed to be sure Dad was going to listen. Dad knew it too. "I have plenty of time."

He took out his phone and switched it off, relaxing into the chair as if he was happy to sit there forever. "Why don't you tell me where it did start?"

Catching sat still and quiet for a while longer. Her gaze drifted in my direction again, although she couldn't be really seeing me.

Then she said, "It started with a sunset."

Catching

THE SUNSET

We're on top of a rocky hill.
      Mum's hair is redder than the setting sun.
"I told you not to trust a color called Scarlet Dream," I say.
She grins. "How do you feel, Izzy?"
"Cold."
Mum's knitting is as bad as her hair dye.
My jumper's long, but it's not warm.

She puts her jacket over my shoulders.
"Now?"
"Warmer."
"Calmer?"
I nod. Calmer.
More than back home.
Where people are mean. Unfair. And I'm angry.
I'm not good with anger.
It lights my blood like flames.
I become fire.

But on this road trip, Mum's taught me words that
control fire.

The names of the Catching women, from my Great-Great-
Grandma onward.
Granny Trudy Catching . . .
Nanna Sadie Catching . . .
Grandma Leslie Catching . . .
Mum . . .
Me.

I don't say their names out loud.
We don't speak the names of the dead.
So I say them in my mind.
And in my heart, I can breathe.

I always knew Catching women were strong.
But I didn't know what they'd been through.
Not everything.
Not until Mum told me on this trip.
"Catching women are fighters," Mum says. "We've had to
be, to survive. And all the strengths of the Catching women
flow down the family line and into you, Izzy."

I bury my face in her jacket.
She smiles.
The sky rumbles.
Her smile dies.
"It's not supposed to rain today. We need to go!"
We climb down the rocky hill. Race to the car.
The land here is flat.
It floods when it rains.

Mum starts the car. "Seat belt!"

Rain falls.

We bump over rough ground. Back to the road.

Lightning flashes. Thunder roars.

The rain falls harder.

The windscreen wipers can't keep up.

Mum turns on the headlights, but they're useless.

The storm swallows everything.

We can't see.

The highway. Where is it?

A wall of water smashes into the car.

The river!

My head slams against the window.

My eyes close.

Time passes.

My eyes open.

Someone's shouting. Mum.

She's tugging at my seat belt. Trying to get it undone.

She's reaching round a tree to do it.

There's a tree growing in the car. Weird.

Not weird. It's a branch.

The front window is shattered.

Water pours in.

Mum shouts again. I can't understand her.

The water is up to my chest . . .

My neck . . .

My chin . . .
Mum's eyes meet mine.
Her lips move.
One last word.
Water swallows me whole.

The seat belt clicks.
The current sweeps me away.
Mum!

My head spins.
My arms and legs won't work.
I'm going to die.
All the strengths of the Catching women flow down the family
line and into you.
That matters.
Nanna Sadie. There's something about her I've got to
remember.

My lungs scream for air.
I'm lost in the dark of the water.
No up and no down.

Words shine in the dark beneath my feet.
They speak in Mum's voice.

When your Nanna was little, the government took her
away from her mum. They had a law back then that

let them take Aboriginal kids just because they were
Aboriginal . . .

Her voice wouldn't lead me wrong.
Down is up!
I turn in the water.
I follow the words.

They stuck her on a ship. She was going to a bad place.
But the government people didn't know about your Nanna's
strength with water. She was born in a big storm, and when
she cried for the first time, a sound like thunder came out her
mouth.

My mouth opens.
It wants air.
It fills with water. I'm choking!
I roar.
A sound like thunder pushes the water out.

She jumped off that ship into the waves and swam. First
through the sea until she reached the shore, then through one
river after another, all the way back to her mum.

Your Nanna could swim like a fish.

My legs move.
I kick.

Once. Twice.
Again.
I swim like a fish.
I swim like my Nanna.

I burst through the surface.

Breath heaves.
In.
Out.
It burns. I keep gulping air.

Rain still falls.
I'm being dragged by the current.
My arm hits something. A tree?

I grab hold.
Not a tree.
A root, attached to a tree on the riverbank.
I claw my way up.

Lightning tears the sky.
There's a shape lying on the shore.
Mum!
I stagger over.
The lightning fades.
I reach her in the dark. Drop to my knees.
"Mum, wake up!"

Lightning flashes.
Mum's eyes are open.
Staring.
But not *seeing*.

I press my finger to her neck.
No pulse.

She's dead.

THE OTHER-PLACE

I cry until the lightning dies.
I scream until the thunder fades.
I howl into the dirt.
Give her back!
But the earth stays silent.
Soon I'm silent too.
I fall to the ground. My eyes close.

I don't want to wake . . .
But I do.

Everything is strange.
Two suns hang in the air.
There's no river. Only a stream.
The trees have no leaves. They crowd together in a forest of
sticks.
All the colors are washed away.
The sky is gray, not blue.
The trees are dull, not white.
Even the suns are pale.

Where Mum's body was is an empty space.
She's gone.

Impossible.
Her body was right there.

I stand. Pat the earth as if it has eaten her.
Nothing.
Maybe her body hasn't gone anywhere. Maybe *I* have.
Somewhere different. Somewhere *else*.

My head throbs. I put my hand on it.
There's something grainy matted in my hair.
Blood.

I'm hurt. Alone.
In some other-place.
I should be scared.
But I'm not.
Mum's gone. Nothing else matters.
Memories stab my brain.
Us on that hill. The storm. The drive. The water.
She said something to me.
Just one word.
Right before she unclipped my seat belt.
I couldn't hear it then.
I can now.
Live.

I fall back to the ground.
My heart is hollow.
Empty.
My body is heavy.
Weak.
Maybe I'll fade away . . .
Like the colors of this place.
Yet I don't.

Live.

My throat tightens.
Tears run.
The last thing she did was save me.
She asked for one thing.

Live.

I don't want to.
But I've got to.

I stand. The world spins.
I stab a leg out. Catch my balance.
Pain spikes through my head.
I stagger to the stream. Gulp down water.
There are fish darting about.
Food.

I walk back to the trees.
Break off a branch.
File the end against a rock.
Spear.

I wade into the water.
The fish flee, only to come back as the ripples die.
I hurl my spear.
It stabs the sandy bed.
Misses the fish.
I reach for it.
Lift. Aim. Throw.
Miss.

My stomach growls.
So does something else.

There are things in the distance.
Things that shimmer in the air like they're made of water.
They've each got four legs. One tail.
Big jaws that hang open to show gleaming teeth.
Muscles that ripple as they paw the ground.

I grip my spear.
But there are too many to fight.

One of them yips.
All of them charge.

I run into the stick forest.
The shimmer beasts chase after me.
They howl, surrounding me with wails.
Terror sends strength flowing through my legs.
Something flashes beside me.
I lash out. A beast yelps.
I keep running.
The howls fade.
Then the trees stop.

No more forest. Just a rocky cliff wall.
I look left. Right. The wall goes on forever.
They've herded me here.

Live.

I drop the spear and climb.
The world shrinks to edges and angles.
Reach up. Grab the rock. Pull.
Find a hole—there!
Dig in your foot. Stretch . . .
Howls sound beneath me.
I glance over my shoulder.
The beasts pace below.
One bites down on my spear.
The others fight over the remains.
Snap. Snarl. Claw. Rip.

They'll eat me the same way.

I keep going.
My muscles hurt.
My fingers tremble.
I'm almost there.
I can see the top of the cliff!
But there's no way to reach it.
I've hit smooth, flat rock.

I search for a hold. Find none.
There's a ledge to my right. I could rest there. Work out
what to do.
I stretch my body as far as it can go.
Not far enough.
Can't go down. Can't go up.
That ledge is my only chance.
It's out of reach. Unless I jump.

I take a breath.
Focus on the ledge.
Jump.

For a second, I'm a bird.
A cloud.
A leaf in the breeze.
Then my right hand claws at the rock.
My fingers dig into a hollow.
My body swings outward.
My hand stretches . . . *Snap.*

I scream but don't let go.

I slam my other hand into the hole too.
Pain tears down my arm.
It doesn't want to hold on.
I suck in air. One breath. Two.
Up!
I shoot over the ledge.

My chest lands on top. My legs kick open air.
I swing them onto rock.
My body shakes. My hand hurts.
But I'm safe. For now.

Almost falling taught me something.
The voice that told me to live . . .
This time, it wasn't just Mum's.
It was mine too.

I close my eyes.
The wind blows across my bruised body.
For a moment, everything stills.
Pauses.
Rests.
Then sounds echo in the rush of air.
Voices.
Somebody's talking, somewhere above.

My eyes blink open.
"Hello?" I call.

No answer.

I stand, try again. "Hello? Anyone there?"

"It speaks," a voice hisses.

"All girls speak," another answers.

"Yes. Speak. Scream. Cry."

Two figures appear on the clifftop above.

Then they jump off.

I wait for them to fall past me.

Instead, they . . . flap? . . . onto the ledge.

They've got *wings*. Leathery. Gray.

Their robes are gray too.

Long robes, which hide their heads and bodies.

Robes that blend with everything else and make their edges hard to see.

Their faces are covered by white masks with human features.

But they can't be human.

Calling out was a *bad* idea.

They don't feel right.

Not because they're strange-looking.

It's something else.

A wrongness that makes the hairs on the back of my neck prickle.

I want my spear.

"What are you?" I demand.

They answer together, "Fetchers."

One points to himself. "*I* am he-who-is-First."
He points to the other. "This is he-who-is-Second."
First is larger. First is *first*. The boss.
Boss people want everyone to know they're in charge.

"She has colors," Second says.
"Bright," First agrees. "Beautiful. Like a rainbow."
Second hops toward me. "Are you alone, little rainbow?"
Fear stirs my stomach.
"No," I lie. "I'm here with my mum."
Who's dead.
"My dad."
Who took off with another woman years ago.
"Lots of people."
First goes quiet. Tilts his head. Listens.
Laughs. "*Liar.* No parents, no nothing. You're a lost little
rainbow."

I back up until I hit the cliff.
"Don't worry," Second says. "We make lost things found.
We'll make you found too."
"We'll *fetch* you," First agrees.
"Stay back!" I snap.
But they're not afraid.
I'm small, and they're big.
They have wings that fly.
Claws that fetch.
I have only me.

My eyes never leave the Fetchers.
But my hands search the wall.
Looking for a rock. A weapon. Anything!
I find nothing.

They come closer.
I hear a sniff behind the mask. "She's damaged."
Second doesn't sound happy.
Maybe damaged is bad?
Bad for them is good for me.

"I'm hurt," I say. "Broke my hand. Smashed my head. I'm all
messed up."
"She can be fixed," First says.
"Only to be broken?" Second asks.
First shrugs. "Not our job. Our job is to fetch. To mend. To
give to *him*."
Second nods.
First lunges.
I swing my fist. Kick my feet. Yell.
It's useless.

The not-human thing is larger than me.
Faster than me.
Stronger than me.

I'm fetched.

THE BENEATH

We soar over the stick forest.
I don't fight.
I've got no wings.
If I get free, I'll fall.

First circles in the air.
Below is a boulder. It looks like an egg tipped on its side.
Across from it is a tree.
Between the two is dirt.

We plunge toward the dirt.

My stomach slams into my throat.
My skin pushes back from my face.
The earth opens like a mouth.

We're swallowed.

I'm dropped to the floor. I get up. Stagger in the gray gloom.
My hand slaps against cold rock. *Wall.*

But wall runs into floor. Floor runs into ceiling.
Tunnel.
Second speaks to First: "We must tell him we have fetched."
"*I* will tell him. You will fix her."
Second's wings dip in disappointment.
"You are good at fixing," First says. "You will make her shiny and new."
Second draws himself up. Proud.
My stomach twists.
I'm a doll.
I'm a prize.
For *him*.
The real boss. First is only the boss of Second.

There's someone else.

Second grabs my arm.
I'm dragged along.
I don't fight.
Right now there's no way out.
So I save my strength. Wait for my chance.
Ahead is a door.
It's gray like everything else.
Second shoves it open. Pushes me inside.

I see shelves.
They hold clear cubes of jelly.
Can't be jelly.

Something else.
The door shuts.
A lock clicks.
I'm trapped.

Second leaps. I jump back.
Raise my hands.
The broken one can't make a fist.
Can't defend me.
But Second just flaps over my head.

He lands by a shelf. Grabs two cubes and tosses them in
the air.
A metal hand drops from above, catching the cubes.
More hands dangle from the ceiling.
The cubes are thrown back and forth.
Smashed together.
Pulled apart.
Second is watching the hands.

My eyes search the room.
Looking for a weapon . . . a way out . . . anything.
But there's nothing.
Mum's voice speaks inside my head: *Knowledge can be a
weapon, Iz.*
She said that to get me to go to school.
Doesn't mean it isn't true.
Second's not as smart as First.
Maybe he'll let something slip?

"What is this place?" I ask.

"This is where we bring the colors."

"I'll give you some of my colors if you help me get out."

Second laughs. High-pitched. Grating.

"Colors are not for Fetchers! We find. We give. But never keep. Colors are for him."

"Who's 'him'?"

"He is the one who takes the colors."

Useless.

There's a hissing sound from above.

The hands disappear into a cloud of steam.

Something drops.

Same jelly. Different shape. A sphere instead of a cube.

Second plucks it out of the air. "Medicine!"

He bounces over.

I back up.

He snorts impatiently and slaps the sphere onto my broken hand.

I try to scrape it off.

There's nothing to scrape.

It's sunk through my skin.

It burns.

First my outside. Then my inside.

I drop.

Twist.

Scream.

The burning shrinks.
Smaller and smaller until it's nothing.
I sit up.
There's no pain. Not anywhere.
I make a fist. It doesn't hurt.
I touch my head. Unbroken skin.
Medicine.

Second looms above me. Another sphere drops onto my arm.
I try to shake it off. Too late. It's part of me.
But there's no burning this time.
Only fuzziness.

Second hauls me out the door.
I try to track where we're going.
I can't.
Everything joins together in grayness. It's all tunnels. Until
it's not.
I'm in a room. A big room? A small one?
I don't know. Sleep is dragging at me.
The world is fading.

The Fetcher dumps me onto the floor.
Not the floor. A bed.
My head hits a pillow.
He leaves.

I fight to stay awake.
I lose.

Beth

THE TRUTHS

Catching stopped speaking. Just stopped, and turned away from us to stare out the window at the long shadows of the late afternoon.

Monsters and other-places. Other dimensions. It was all so unbelievable, and yet what she'd said felt true. And after all, I was living proof that there was more to the world than what most people saw. Okay . . . not *living* proof. But proof just the same.

Only we still didn't know how Catching had ended up back in this dimension on the night of the fire.

"You can't stop there!" I blurted out. "How did you escape?"

Of course my words had no effect on her. I looked at Dad. "Ask her what happened next!"

But all my father said to Catching was: "Talked enough for today, huh? That's all right. I'll come again another time."

What was he doing? We hadn't even got to the fire, which was why he'd come here in the first place! But then Catching turned toward us, and I saw that her eyes were sunken and her cheeks hollow. Shame prickled over my skin. I should have noticed that it was hurting her to tell the story. Dad clearly had.

He rose and offered her a smile. "Is there someone you want me to contact for you? A relative, perhaps?"

"Worried I'm all alone?" Her lips twisted into a snarl that said *back off* as clearly as if she'd shouted it. "Don't be. I got somebody."

I could see Dad would've liked to ask who but wasn't going to push her. I trailed behind him as he strode to the door, pausing when I reached it to glance back at Catching. I wanted to make sure she was okay.

She was looking right at me.

No, she wasn't. She was looking through me at my father. I suppressed an urge to wave at her and turned my back, ducking through the door as it started to swing shut.

I never walked through doors or walls around Dad. It was just another reminder for him that I was dead. Besides, I needed to hold on to what it had been like to be alive. I was worried that if I lost my sense of the world being solid, I'd start drifting through everything like . . . um, a ghost.

There were fewer patients in the waiting area now, and the only nurse at the station was the blond woman we'd talked to before. She sat up straight as Dad approached and spoke in a tone bright with curiosity: "You were in there awhile! Was she helpful? Her memory of that night is a bit spotty."

The remaining patients shifted a little toward us, straining to hear Dad's response.

The corner of Dad's mouth turned up. He knew they were all hoping for a bit of news to share with their families about the big fire. He wasn't going to give it to them, of course. He was too good a police officer for that. Instead, he said, "Seems like she could use some family support. Has anyone been in to see her?"

The nurse shook her head. "Child services has only just managed to locate her mother. The girl's a runaway from a rehab clinic in the city. Her mum should be here in about a week to take her back."

That was impossible, and I half expected Dad to say as much. But he just thanked her and strolled toward the front door, leaving the nurse and patients to stare after him in disappointment.

"Why are you leaving?" I demanded. "They can't be taking proper care of Catching if they don't even realize her mum's dead!"

Dad didn't respond until he was standing in the empty car park. Then he said, "Catching's mum isn't dead."

"She drowned in the river!"

"I don't think so, Beth."

I stared at him in confusion. How could he have heard what I'd heard and yet not felt the realness of it? "Catching wasn't lying. I know she wasn't."

"I don't think she was lying, precisely. Just telling the truth in a different way."

"What's that supposed to mean?"

"Well . . . take the shimmer beasts. If you look at the

53

horizon when it's hot, it can shimmer. She was wandering around for a day before she was found, probably thirsty and disorientated. So the shimmering horizon becomes a horde of shimmer beasts chasing after her."

I frowned. "Okay, but you really think she imagined her mum dying?"

"If her mum was the one who put her into the rehab clinic, Catching could've felt abandoned, turned those feelings into a story about death. And there *was* a big storm a few months back. It was on the news, remember? It caused all that property damage. Except no one was killed in it."

He was starting to make sense. But I wasn't giving up yet. "What about the other-place? And the Fetchers?"

"When your life gets upended—like when you're admitted to rehab, say—it can feel like you've been thrown into a strange place. And she would have been given medicine by the people who worked at the clinic."

"But the medicine hurt!"

"Coming off drugs does hurt, Beth."

Oh. Catching had taken a bunch of events and woven them into a story, and, like Dad had said, it wasn't exactly a lie.

But nor was it exactly true. And I felt really stupid for having believed that it was.

Dad reached for his phone, staring down at the screen. "Message," he muttered, pushing a button and holding the phone to his ear. After a few moments, he let out an exasperated sigh.

"What is it?" I asked.

"Bank accounts," he answered as he shoved the phone back into his pocket. "Tom Cavanagh's and Martin Flint's. We've been checking on their credit card activity and withdrawals, hoping to trace Cavanagh's movements. Or even Flint's, if by some small chance it turns out he didn't die in the fire. And they both seem to have more money than they should."

I didn't see why that was a problem. "So?"

"So they could have been embezzling from the home. Which explains why Cavanagh ran." He gave a frustrated shake of his head. "It's just as I thought from the start—this is a waste of my time. Faulty wiring starts the fire, which gets out of control fast, the way fires do. Cavanagh realizes there'll be an investigation and takes off. Flint is overcome by smoke. And a mixed-up teenage runaway from the city is found while people are searching for the director."

He yanked his keys from his pocket and headed for the car.

"Where are you going now?" I demanded.

"Hotel."

Where he'd probably sink into sadness now that he didn't have the case to think about.

"Why don't you get some food?" I asked. "There was that café on the main street. It might still be open."

"Not hungry."

He hadn't eaten since this morning, and my Uncle Kelvin wasn't around to turn up at the door with one of his delicious stews and all of his best jokes. Uncle Kel hadn't managed to get Dad to laugh yet, but he always got him to eat. Here, though, there was nobody to take care of Dad but me.

"Have a sandwich or something," I pleaded.

He didn't even bother to respond, just kept trudging wearily toward the car. In desperation, I called after him, "*Talk* to me, Dad! I'm right here."

He paused, with his hand on the door, and spoke without looking at me. "No, Beth. You're not."

Then he got into the sedan and drove away.

"I am!" I yelled. "I'm always here!"

But my voice was swallowed by the sound of the engine as my father zoomed off into the distance. I was alone. Well, *more* alone, actually, since I'd already been feeling that way before he left. It didn't seem right that I could sometimes feel so isolated around my father and yet always so much a part of everything around the rest of the family, when he was the one who could see me.

Nothing ever went how it was supposed to. Like this case, which I'd really thought might change things for Dad. Now everything was ruined.

Catching shouldn't have lied to us.

It was dumb to be mad at her. But I was. I was mad that she'd fooled me with her story. And I was mad that she hadn't given Dad hope that there was more to this case. As long as she was inventing things, she could've invented something about the fire that would've made him think there was a real mystery to solve. That was illogical, and I knew it, but I didn't care.

I stalked back into the hospital, so angry that I didn't think twice about charging through walls and doors to get to Catching. I stormed up to the end of her bed and opened my mouth to yell at her.

She looked right at me. "Took you long enough."

I choked on my words, producing meaningless spluttering sounds, until I finally managed to put together a sentence. "You can *see* me?"

She rolled her eyes.

"How can you see me? No one else can except Dad!"

Catching yawned, as if talking to ghosts was no big deal. "My mum could see people who'd passed over."

Which meant Catching could too. Because all the strengths of the Catching women flow down the family line and into her.

I couldn't believe it. Someone besides my father could see me. Was *talking* to me. This was so enormous that I didn't know what to say.

Catching didn't have that problem. "Did your dad kill you?"

I gaped at her. "Wh— Of course not! That's a horrible thing to say."

"Why're you haunting him, then?"

"I'm not. I'm looking after him."

"So who killed you?"

I shrugged. "Some guy who lost control of his car in the rain. I died in a stupid accident."

She frowned. "But you're stuck."

"No, I'm not."

"You're still here, aren't you? Like you've got unfinished business. If you weren't murdered, why are you so crap at being dead?"

"I am not! Besides, there's no good way to be dead."

"Yeah, there is. It's called moving on. To what's next."

"Um, maybe this is my 'what's next.'"

"Can't be, because it's your what *was*. You never got a call to go somewhere else?"

"No, I . . ." But I couldn't finish that sentence. Because there had been something, right after I'd died. A glimpse of something that dazzled and danced—like light, refracting through crystal. I'd been going to those colors until I'd heard my dad crying for me.

Catching was watching my face. "Let me guess. You *were* going somewhere else. Then you decided it was a better idea to trail around after that sad old man."

I glared at her. "He's not a sad old man!"

"He looked pretty miserable to me."

"Well, I mean obviously he's a bit sad, after everything."

Catching opened her eyes wide and spoke in a sugary tone: "Did something terrible happen to him?" Then her eyes narrowed and the sweetness vanished from her voice. "No, wait—something terrible happened to *you*. You're the one who died."

"It happened to him too!" I didn't like what she was saying. I especially didn't like that a tiny part of me thought she might have a point.

My anger bubbled back up, setting me on fire with a strange fizzing heat that seemed to pop and ripple along my skin.

"You don't know anything about him. But I know about you, Isobel Catching. You were never in an other-place, and your mum's not even dead either. She just threw you into rehab."

The heat leaped into my throat to crackle out of my mouth.

"So you'd better just take care of your own life *and leave me and my dad alone!*"

The light in the ceiling exploded.

I yelped in surprise. Catching dived under the bed, sheltering there until the sparks had faded and the glass had stopped falling.

"Are you okay?" I asked as she came back out.

"Yeah." She shook out the blanket, sending a few tiny slivers skittering along the floor, and climbed onto the mattress. "No thanks to you."

"I did that?"

But I knew I had. I'd felt the energy surge out of my body and into the room. I just didn't quite believe it.

"Do you know *how* I did that?"

"Spirits can do things like that sometimes, when they're really mad. Or happy or sad, or whatever. So my mum said."

I gazed up at the remains of the light in astonishment. I'd never blown anything up before. On the other hand, I'd never been that angry before—or at least not since right after I'd died.

Except now my anger was gone, emptied out of me and into the light. And without the rage to cloud my thinking, I realized something.

Catching believed my father was bad for me. First because she'd thought he'd hurt me, and then because she'd decided he was the reason I hadn't moved on to "what's next." She was trying to help. She just had her own unique way of going about it.

"Sorry," I said. "For yelling and everything."

She shrugged as if she didn't care whether I was sorry or not, but I could tell she was pleased. "What's your name, ghost girl?"

"Beth. Beth Teller."

An almost-smile pulled at the corner of her mouth. "Guess you have a strange name too. White boss give it to your family?"

I shook my head. "It's not Mum's name; it's Dad's. I don't think it means anything, except . . . I guess Dad is kind of a teller. Someone who tells what's right from what's wrong, that is."

Or at least he had been. Before I'd died, Dad had always been the one I'd gone to when I didn't know what to do about something. Only now it was him who couldn't see what was right. Like calling Aunty Viv. I guessed that made me the teller now.

But he wasn't listening to me.

My gaze slid back up to what was left of the light. "Catching? Did your mum ever say if someone who was, um, stuck like me could touch people? Like, hug them, or . . . or hold their hand?"

She snorted. "That's your plan now? Hang about and hold your dad's hand for the rest of his life?"

"No. Not exactly." Even I could hear the lie in my voice.

She pointed to the door. "Get out of here, Teller. Come back if you ever want help doing what you're supposed to be doing and *move on.*"

"Catching—"

"Go!" she shouted.

I faded out of the hospital before she got any madder. I'd have to wait until she calmed down before I saw her again. Except I didn't want her help to move on. The help I needed was to stay.

I turned my steps in the direction of the hotel Dad had checked into that morning. I didn't actually need to walk to the place, because if I focused on Dad, I'd arrive at wherever he was. But I knew if I took long enough getting there, he'd be asleep, and that was a good thing. It meant I wouldn't have to watch him crying. So I made a meandering journey through the town, wandering past a post office, a set of shops, and a school. I didn't see many people, and once it got properly dark, there were none. Just me and the stars and a few crows calling out in the night.

The hotel was called Lakeview, because the upstairs rooms in the old weatherboard part of the building had a view of a lake to the back. Dad's room was in the newer brick extension and had a view of the road.

I phased into the room, relieved to find him sprawled across the bed and snoring. He'd left the lamp on. The soft glow shone across features that were slack and sunken, as if he was caving in on himself.

He didn't look like my dad. He didn't look like he was together enough to be anyone's dad.

Catching's unwelcome voice echoed in my memory: *That's your plan now? Hang about and hold your dad's hand for the rest of his life?*

For a treacherous moment, I found myself wondering if there was something better for me than this grinding struggle to get my father back to himself. But I stomped on that thought, jamming it down into the depths of my being, where it belonged. He needed me. And I had a new way to help him. If I could figure out how to touch the world again, it'd change everything for Dad; I just knew it. Maybe I'd be able to reach the rest of the family too. I could just see their smiling faces . . .

Only I couldn't. All I could really see was Aunty June's frizzy eyebrows drawn together in a frown and her black curls bouncing as she shook her head at me.

Aunty June had always called me her butterfly girl, because I lived in the now, leaving behind the things that weighed me down the way butterflies left their caterpillar selves. Aunty had said I was always who I was today and never who I'd been yesterday, and that my mum had been the same. I liked that; it had made me feel closer to the mother I couldn't remember.

Except I didn't feel like a butterfly girl anymore. I was heavy with the weight of lifting up my father, and I knew Aunty wouldn't want that for me. I didn't feel like a teller either. I couldn't tell what the right thing was to do, or at least not the right thing for myself.

And in the silence of this drab hotel room, the future, where I could make things right again for my caved-in father, seemed a long way away.

I huddled down by the bed, wrapping my arms around my legs, and I did the thing I never did when Dad was awake to see it.

I cried.

THE STATION

Daylight shone through the gap in the curtains. I hadn't slept, because I didn't anymore. But in between when I'd stopped crying and now, I'd made a plan.

When Dad woke up, I was going to tell him Catching could see me. That would get him interested in Catching again, which would get him interested in the case again. And her story might have more truth to it than Dad thought. Her gaze was so deep, like there was no end to the things she'd seen. She didn't seem like someone who'd run away from a rehab facility and lost her way among trees and rocks. She seemed like someone whose mum had died and who'd been hunted by shimmer beasts and kidnapped by Fetchers. If anything that terrible, or even close to that terrible, had happened, then I was sure Dad could help her, and helping her would help him too.

The only problem was that talking to Catching might make Dad sadder, especially if she started going on about how I was wasting my "what's next" by following him around. But if I didn't find something to spark his interest in the world soon, I was worried he'd slide so far back into the mud that he'd never get out. It wasn't a perfect plan, but it was the only one I had.

Dad's phone rang, buzzing across the top of the table where he'd left it. I went over to check on the name of the caller.

Rachel Ali. Dad's boss.

I dashed to the bed and bent down to shout in his ear. "Wake *up*!"

He jolted upright, blinking at me. "Whaaa . . ."

"Phone, Dad! It's Rachel."

Dad tried to get up and got tangled in the blanket. He shoved it aside and lurched to his feet, knocking his knee against the nightstand. Groaning, he hobbled across the room to grab the phone.

"Hello?"

Rachel started talking. After a moment, Dad responded. "Yeah, Jen left me a message about the money yesterday . . . No, haven't checked in with the locals yet, wanted to get a feel for the place first . . ."

Rachel's voice grew sharp. Dad looked sheepish.

"Well, I went and saw the home—what's left of it, anyway— and I interviewed the witness . . . Yes, I can handle this!"

There was silence on the other end of the line, like Rachel wasn't so sure. Then she spoke again. Dad's eyes widened. "Not the fire? That's confirmed?"

He went quiet, listening with absolute concentration. My hopes rose. Something was going on.

"I'll get the address from the locals," Dad said. "I'm on my way to the station now . . . Yep, I'll keep you posted . . . Bye."

"What's happened?" I demanded as he hung up.

Dad rubbed the sleep out of his eyes. "Remember Martin Flint—well, the person who died, who's probably Martin Flint? Whoever it was, they *didn't* die in the fire. They were stabbed."

"*Stabbed?*"

"With an unusual weapon too—some kind of blade with a slight curve to it. Only nothing like that was found at the scene, so it's still out there somewhere."

A murder. This was . . . well, not good, obviously, but I couldn't help feeling guiltily relieved that there'd been a development in the case, even if it was something horrible.

"What's the address you're supposed to get?" I asked. "A lead on the killer?"

Dad shook his head. "No. The home address of Alexander Sholt."

It took me a second to place the name. "The guy who donated the house and the money to start the home? The pale, skinny one from that photo?"

"That's the one. He had a lot of involvement with the place, and it seems like *something* was going on there—although possibly not embezzlement."

"Why not embezzlement?"

"Because it turns out that Nurse Flint and Director Cavanagh have both been making regular cash deposits into their bank accounts going back years. So it feels more like they were being paid off for something . . . or perhaps they were selling something."

He was silent for a moment, then continued, "The home received medical supplies for the kids, so maybe they were selling prescription meds on the side? Was that why Catching was there, to buy? Except there haven't been any reports of problems with drug trafficking in this area. Could they have kept it that quiet for all that time?"

He went silent again, staring into space with a slight frown between his eyes. This was his thinking face, and I was pleased to see it. But he couldn't keep standing around here.

"We have to go, Dad. You told Rachel you were already on your way to the local station, remember? And you need to take a shower, because you're all rumpled." I pointed toward the bathroom. "Get moving!"

A hot shower and two cups of coffee later, we were driving through the town. He didn't look too bad, considering.

I hadn't told Dad that Catching could see me. I didn't need to anymore. He was definitely going to talk to her again now that this was a confirmed homicide, though, and I realized I was hoping she wouldn't tell him either. It wasn't just because I didn't want her hurting him. Since I'd died, my only link to the world of the living had been Dad. Now I had someone else, and deep where I buried the things I didn't like to acknowledge, I had to admit that I liked having a connection that was mine alone. It was almost as if I had a friend.

Dad rolled the car to a halt outside the station. Unsurprisingly, it was a large weatherboard with a big veranda and a sign out front that said POLICE.

"Rachel was mad at you for not coming here yesterday, huh?"

"I should have," Dad conceded. "But when I saw the town, and it reminded me so much of where I grew up . . ." He shrugged. "I just wanted to take a look at things on my own first. Small towns can be like lakes: quiet and still on the surface, but with lots going on beneath."

"Like a secret international drugs conspiracy!"

Dad chuckled. "Drugs, maybe. International conspiracy— probably not."

A laugh. I'd got him to laugh, and without it making him sad afterward, like it had yesterday. It was going to be a good day, I just knew it.

I hugged the sound of the laugh to myself all the way into the station and into the office of the man in charge.

The boss of the police here had mousy blond hair and hazel eyes, and didn't seem very pleased to see Dad. He stood as Dad entered his office. "Detective Teller? I'm Derek Bell."

Dad held out his hand, and Bell shook it reluctantly. Then Dad settled into the chair in front of the desk, casting a quick glance around as he did so. I did as well, but there wasn't much to see: a big window that gave a view of sky and trees and crows, and a bookcase containing a bunch of files and a few photos. One of the photos showed Derek Bell as a teenager, standing with a tall man in a police uniform. His dad? Maybe policing ran in the family.

Dad opened his mouth to speak, but Bell got in first: "I hear you've been going around town asking questions."

How did he know that? Had he been following us yesterday? I eyed him with suspicion. Maybe he was part of the conspiracy I was hoping existed.

Dad laughed. "Small-town grapevine working as well as ever, I see. I should have dropped by yesterday—sorry! Just trying to get a jump on the work."

Bell's mouth pressed into a thin line. "I don't know how you do things in the city, but here it's considered common courtesy to check in with us before you go conducting witness interviews and the like."

There was a whining edge to his voice that made it hard to take him seriously. He sounded less like a stern police officer and more like a little kid complaining that his big brother had stolen his ice cream.

Dad sighed. "Look, when I get back home, my boss is going to ask, 'Did you look at the crime scene?' So I looked at the scene. Then she's going to ask, 'Did you talk to the witness?' So I talked to the witness."

He leaned forward and spoke in a low tone of voice, as if he was sharing a secret: "You don't need me telling you how to do your job. I know how hard policing in a small town can be. Grew up in a place not much bigger than this myself. My dad was the local cop."

Bell softened. "Really? Mine too."

Dad made a show of surprise, but I knew he'd noticed the photo when he looked around the room. My father was the one who'd taught me how to scan a space for the details that

69

told you things about the person who occupied it. *Way to put the guy at ease, Dad.*

Bell relaxed back into his chair. "I don't suppose you got anything out of that witness? She didn't have anything useful to say when she talked to my people, but I hear you were with her awhile."

That treacherous nurse must have gossiped to Bell.

Dad just shrugged. "Kid didn't have anything useful to say to me either, unless you count tales of the general unfairness of her existence. Teenagers!"

I bristled. Then I saw Bell's shoulders sag in relief—he'd been more interested in the answer to that question than he'd let on. And Dad had . . . well, kind of lied to him, or at least diverted him away from Catching.

Derek Bell was a suspect.

I studied him with renewed interest, taking in the bags under his eyes and the way his nails were bitten down to the quick. Something was worrying this man.

"Look, I have to get an address," Dad said. "For an Alexander Sholt."

Bell stiffened. "Alex?"

"Friend of yours?" Dad asked. His tone was pleasant, but I wasn't fooled. I could see how closely he was watching Derek Bell.

"We were at school together," Bell replied. "But everyone around here knows the Sholt family. They donate a lot of funds to local causes. You want to speak to Alex about the home?"

Dad nodded. "We'll need to dig deeper into the place now that it's a homicide, and Sholt hasn't been returning phone calls. You've been briefed on the autopsy results?"

"Got the call this morning." Bell swallowed, looking queasy. "Last time there was a killing in this town, it was a bar fight gone wrong—nothing like this. Um, you surely don't think Alex could be involved . . ."

"I'm just looking for a better sense of the home and the people who worked there. Seems like Alexander Sholt might be able to give me that."

Did Bell seem relieved? It was hard to be sure with all his general twitchiness, but I thought so.

"I'll get you his address," he said. "But I don't think you'll have much luck. Alex lives here part of the time, but he also has a flat in the city, and I haven't seen him around town lately."

"His city address was checked this morning. His neighbor said she thought he was here."

Bell blinked in surprise. "Did she? Well, perhaps he is. He does go back and forth." He paused for a second, eyes narrowed in thought, and then said, "I tell you what, the Sholt house can be a bit hard to find; I'll get my second-in-command to take you."

"There's really no need—"

"It's no trouble." He rose and strode to the door. "Back in a sec!"

As he left, I said to Dad, "Did you see how stressed out he is? I think he and Sholt are *both* dodgy and totally in league

71

with each other. Bell probably covered up the others' selling the drugs—that's how they could have kept it quiet."

Dad answered softly, "That's possible. Although it seems like the Sholt family has enough money already, without needing to get tangled up in criminal activities."

"Unless crime is where the Sholts got all their money in the first place! Either way, Bell is hiding something."

"He's nervy, but that doesn't necessarily mean he knowingly covered something up." Dad's mouth tightened. "It seems to me he might be a little like my father—the kind of cop who thinks the rules don't apply to everyone equally. He could've been too deferential to the Sholt family, given them special treatment . . . maybe let a few things slide about that home that he sees he should have looked into. If so, it'll all come out now, and he knows it."

Well, that was disappointing. I wanted Derek Bell to be a dastardly criminal mastermind, not a weaselly and incompetent official. Although I had to admit, "weaselly" and "incompetent" fit him better.

"If you don't think Bell's covering things up, why'd you steer him away from Catching?" I asked.

"Because I don't know how deep Alexander Sholt's involvement goes in whatever's been happening, and I don't trust Bell not to let something slip. And Catching . . ." Dad sighed. "I'm not sure if she saw anything that night. I'm not sure if she even remembers it. But if she does have something to say, it's best she says it to me."

There were footsteps outside and Bell returned, followed

by a woman with short red hair, freckles, and a wide smile. Dad rose as they entered and reached across to shake the woman's hand. "Michael Teller."

"Allison Hartley. Call me Allie!"

"Allie will take you to the Sholt place," Bell said. "I'd run you over myself, but I have my hands full, managing the search for Tom Cavanagh."

"Any sign of him?" Dad asked.

"Nothing yet. But I'll let you know if there are any developments."

I followed behind Bell as he walked Dad and Allison-call-me-Allie back through the station and out the front door. Then I lingered as my father and Allie disappeared into the distance, curious to see what Bell would do when Dad's back was turned. Stare balefully after Dad? Mutter to himself about his nefarious plans? Okay, that last one was unlikely, but I could hope.

Except Bell didn't pay any attention to my father. Instead, he peered up and down the street, almost as if he expected to find someone watching him. The wind tossed a can along the pavement, making it clatter when it hit the ground. Bell jumped at the sound, clutching hold of the doorframe. He cast another anxious glance around, then scuttled back inside.

Huh.

Weaselly and incompetent, maybe.

But also afraid.

THE MISSING

We motored through the streets in Allie's car, with Dad up front and me perched in the middle of the back seat. Allie talked as she drove. She talked a *lot,* and in a tone of voice I could only have described as "sunshiny." This woman was the most cheerful cop I'd ever met.

Finally Dad interrupted the steady flow of bright chatter to ask, "Did you grow up around here?"

"I've lived here all my life."

"You must have been at school with Alexander Sholt and Derek Bell, then."

Allie nodded. "I was, although they were a few years ahead of me. And Alex was at boarding school for a while. He came back to the local school when the money problems started."

"I didn't think the Sholt family had any money problems."

"They don't now. But back then, Oscar Sholt—Alex's grandfather—frittered a lot of their fortune away."

"Gambling?"

She laughed. "Nope. The apocalypse!"

Dad blinked. "What?"

"Oscar Sholt thought the end of the world was nigh. He spent thousands on the most ridiculous things—I heard he invested in a colony on the moon. Then he ended up shutting himself away in that old house—the one that became the kids' home later—with a bunch of supplies, to wait out the destruction of civilization as we knew it."

I leaned forward. "So Alexander Sholt *did* have a reason to be tempted to make some illegal cash—at least back while his family had money issues."

Dad grunted in acknowledgment, then said to Allie, "How'd they get the money back?"

"Alex took over the family finances after his grandpa died and turned it all around. He made a lot of cash on the stock market."

I snorted. "Or he made his money selling prescription meds. Or, I don't know, getting involved in some other criminal activity."

Dad shrugged his shoulders, which meant *maybe*.

Allie prattled on: "Alex has done a lot of good in this town—supports the football team, funded the new gym at the school. He's done a lot for those children as well, through the home. He had a bit of a fight on his hands to get it set up too."

Well, that was interesting. Dad thought so as well. "There was some controversy?"

"Some locals didn't want troubled kids on their doorstep. Only some, mind you—plenty of the town wanted to be part of giving the kids a second chance! Bill Carter was going to teach them horseback riding, and Dolly Westerman—she's a retired schoolteacher—offered to run classes for them, and . . . oh, there were lots of people. April Chang started a sign-up sheet for everyone who wanted to help."

She sighed. "Then old Sam Finch started a sign-up sheet for people who *didn't* want the home here. It all got a bit tense. Someone even egged Sam's pub, although there was never any proof that it was Dolly's granddaughter, whatever he said— Anyway, sorry, that's all ancient history now. The home went ahead, but none of us could volunteer there, of course."

"Why not?" I demanded, just as Dad asked the same question.

"It wasn't allowed. The government has very strict rules about how such places have to be run. No one who wasn't directly employed there was allowed in. We didn't even get to see the kids around town—they weren't supposed to leave the home. Pity."

I looked at Dad. "*Are* there rules like that?"

He gave a tiny shake of his head, and I grinned. "Ha! Sholt was trying to keep people away."

Allie kept talking, oblivious to my input: "I know Alex would've liked to have the town involved, if he could have. He loves this place—it's why he still lives here, even with all his money. I mean, if I had his kind of cash . . ." A rueful smile spread across her face. "Actually, you know, I don't suppose I would leave now."

76

"You would have before?" Dad asked.

"When I was a teenager, I couldn't wait to get out! My best friend and I were going to become astronauts, because we figured outer space was the furthest away we could get from this place."

"So why'd you stay?"

The cheerfulness suddenly vanished from Allie's face.

"It was because of my friend Sarah. Sarah Blue. She disappeared."

"Disappeared?" I choked. "How many people can go missing in one small town?"

Dad must have been wondering the same thing. "When was this?" he asked.

"Oh, it was a long time ago. Twenty years . . . seven months . . . six days. Not that I'm counting!" She tried to laugh, but it broke in the middle. "Sarah just vanished a week before her fifteenth birthday. She got off the bus from school, same as always, but she never made it home."

Twenty years. Not related to this case, then. Like Allie had said, it was a long time ago.

Twenty years, seven months, six days . . . Was Dad going to be like this, decades from now when he talked about me? I didn't want him making my death some kind of depressing mathematical reference point for his life.

"You never found out what happened to her?" Dad asked Allie.

"No. Derek's father was in charge of the investigation. He was convinced she'd run off."

"You didn't think so?"

"No, I didn't, and neither did her parents. Sarah might've talked about going away—we both did—but she would never have left her mum and dad without saying goodbye."

Allie sighed. "They're both dead now. They never did get over losing her. The rest of the family live a long way away; Sarah's parents moved here for work. But I'd really like to be able to tell her family that I've found her, one day."

"You think she's still out there somewhere?"

I guessed that was Dad's nice way of asking if Allie thought Sarah was dead.

"It's been a long time," she acknowledged. "But people have been found before, even after years and years. Derek's always telling me there's no point in searching anymore, but . . ."

She cast an anxious glance at Dad, clearly worried he was going to agree with Derek. She didn't know my father.

"We're police officers," he said, and I heard the pride in his voice. "We never stop looking for the missing."

Allie brightened. "I was actually wondering . . . um, that is, if you're not too busy, I was thinking—"

"I'd be happy to take a look at Sarah's file," Dad told her.

She beamed at him. "Thank you!" she said. Then, "It's in the glove compartment."

I laughed. "Bet she's been carrying that file around ever since she got word there was going to be a senior detective in town, Dad."

He gave a small nod of agreement, reaching for the glove compartment. His eyes were crinkling around the edges the way they did when he was suppressing a smile; he liked the way Allie was fighting for her friend.

I edged farther forward, trying to get a good look at the file as he glanced through it. After a moment, he took out a photo, holding it up as if he was studying the image, so that I could see it as well. *Sarah Blue.* She had long black hair, brown skin, and an expression that seemed to dare the world to get in her way. The Aboriginal girl who wanted to go to the stars.

Dad put the photo back and closed the file. "This all there is? Seems thin, for an investigation into a missing kid."

"You think so too? I tried talking to Gerry Bell about it— he's retired now, spends his time fussing over his garden with his wife—but . . . well, Gerry wasn't very receptive. Derek's always saying his dad did everything he could, and I understand that it was a long time ago and investigations are run differently now, of course. It's just that . . ." She shook her head. "Gerry Bell always thought she'd be back any-time." Her fingers tightened on the steering wheel. "Only she never did come back. Do you think any leads can be found now?"

"It won't be easy," Dad warned. "But it's not impossible. It might be best to return to the beginning: re-interview every-one the police spoke to initially, and try to identify anyone they missed. I can help you do it, if you'd like, after the in-vestigation into the home is done."

A huge grin broke over Allie's face, so bright that it made all her other smiles seem like knockoffs of the genuine article. *Small towns can be like lakes.* So could the people in them. There was a lot more to Allison Hartley than just the sunshine on the surface, and I was a bit embarrassed that I hadn't seen that right away. I'd have to do better than that if I was going to be a detective like Dad when I finished . . . Oh.

I wasn't going to be a detective like Dad when I finished school. I wasn't going to be anything. It was so stupid, but sometimes I forgot I was dead—probably because I didn't really *feel* dead. Except that before the accident I'd been a person of the now, always who I was and never who I'd been. But how could I be that butterfly girl when I was *only* who I'd been, stopped forever at fifteen and a half? Unless I moved on to what was next, I sup—

Where had that thought come from? Catching was getting into my head! I scrabbled for other thoughts, comforting thoughts, and found one fast: okay, joining the police force was out, but I could still learn things; still grow and change. I could still be a butterfly like Mum.

I clung to that idea and made it bigger. Maybe Mum would come from wherever she was to find me, and maybe Dad would be able to see her like he could see me; then we'd be a family together! Something didn't feel right about that, but I ignored the feeling. I'd find Mum and fix Dad, and everything would be okay.

The car rounded a corner onto the base of a steep rise.

Allie pointed to the crest of the hill. "See the house at the top? The big one? That's the Sholt place. Alex built it himself—well, had it built, after his mum died and his dad moved in with him."

The house that Sholt built was a two-story redbrick property that dwarfed the weatherboard homes on either side of it and was surrounded by hedges clipped into the shapes of swans. Derek Bell had described it as "a bit hard to find." He'd lied. The only instructions anyone would need to locate this house were "Look for the ugly brick mansion with the pretentious hedges"—which meant Bell hadn't sent Allie with us as a guide. He'd wanted someone to keep an eye on Dad, and he'd be expecting Allie to report back to him.

Dad had figured it out too: as the car rolled to a halt, he said to Allie, "I'd like to interview Sholt alone. I think he'll be more inclined to take this seriously if he's questioned by someone he doesn't know."

Allie didn't object. In fact, she seemed relieved. *Guess she's in an awkward spot, stuck between her boss and Dad.* Now she could truthfully say she'd been left behind and wouldn't have to tell Bell anything.

I followed Dad as he strode up to the front door and lifted the heavy brass knocker to rap against the paneled wood. No one came. He'd just raised his hand to knock again when the door swung back.

The thin, white-haired old man at the door clearly wasn't in the best of health—his pale skin was sallow and his hands were trembling. But there was absolutely nothing wrong with his ability to glare.

Dad held up his identification, ignoring the angry scowl being directed at him. "I need to speak to Alexander Sholt."

"He's not here. Left for the city early this morning."

"Are you his father?"

The old man gave a short nod. "I'm Charles Sholt. What's it to you?"

Dad's gaze flicked to me, then the house. I understood. He wanted me to check if Alexander was hiding inside.

I darted past old man Sholt and began to search, sprinting through rooms filled with fancy furniture and faded photographs of yet more pale Sholt relatives. There was no sign of Alexander on the ground floor, so I headed up a curving staircase.

It was all bedrooms on this level, decorated in assorted shades of cream and beige that seemed to merge together as I tore on through: boring bedroom . . . another cream bedroom . . . another— Wait.

The curtains in this room were fluttering, stirred by the wind. But the window was closed. Strange. I went over to investigate.

There was no glass in the window. The wooden frame was intact, but the glass was gone. I examined the floor beneath it and found some shards.

Someone broke in? Except there was no balcony, and we were a long way off the ground. A person would have to be exceptionally determined to get up here. Maybe it'd been broken by something thrown from the ground. *A rock?*

I was about to turn away when I noticed a few strands of hair caught in the window frame. Black hair.

An image flashed through my mind of the photo Dad had shown me back at the home. Director Cavanagh had black hair. Had he come here, after the fire? It seemed like a place he might run to, if Alexander had been the one paying him off. Cavanagh would've wanted to tell him about the fire, and that the drugs operation was at risk of being uncovered. And maybe ask for some help to get out of town. Except Cavanagh might not have succeeded in getting away, yet. He could still be somewhere in this house.

I spun away from the window and went charging through the rest of the bedrooms. Nothing. Then I went back downstairs and out into the rear garden, in case someone was hiding in the manicured shrubbery. Nothing there either.

Frustrated, I returned to Dad. He was still talking to Charles Sholt—or, more accurately, Charles Sholt was talking to him, going on about how the police should have better things to do with their time than harass successful businessmen like his son.

"No sign of Alexander," I said to Dad. "But there's a broken window upstairs at the back, with strands of black hair caught in the frame. I think Director Cavanagh was here."

Dad interrupted the old man's rambling. "I'm afraid I have to leave now, but I really do need to talk to your son."

He handed over one of his cards. "Please have him contact me as soon as possible."

Sholt dropped the card onto the floor and shuffled back, letting the door swing shut with a bang.

I stared at Dad in confusion.

"What do you mean you have to go? You should be searching the house. I couldn't look in drawers or anything; there could be all sorts of incriminating evidence hidden away!"

Dad glanced back to the car, where Allie was watching. He pulled out his phone and brought it up to his ear.

"Black hair and a smashed window isn't enough, Beth," he said as we walked away from the house. "The window could have been an accident of some kind; the hair could be anyone's—and besides, how could I have known about it?"

Oh. I hadn't thought of that. "But don't you think it's suspicious?"

"I do, especially combined with the way Alexander Sholt seems to be dodging the police. I just can't get a search warrant yet. But I *can* get people to start looking a lot more closely at the Sholt family."

He gave me an approving nod. "You did good, Beth."

I grinned at him. Today had just gone from a good day to a great day. Not only had I helped Dad, I'd done it *as a ghost*, doing something that I couldn't have done when I was alive.

Maybe I could be a detective after all! Okay, not exactly in the way I'd imagined it when I was alive, but still. *Beth Teller. Ghost detective.* This could be the start of a whole new future for Dad and me—and Mum too, once I found her.

My happy thoughts were interrupted as Allie leaped out of her car and bolted over to us, her phone in her hand and red hair flapping around her face. She skidded to a halt in front of Dad. Her skin was white beneath her freckles, but she kept her voice steady and professional as she said, "They've found two more bodies. Both of them have been stabbed."

THE DEATHS

Allie sped through the town in grim silence. Streets flashed by in a blur of weatherboard houses, gum trees, and crows until we finally stopped at one that looked just like all the others—except for the two police cars. The cops had blocked off the whole road, but they were mostly gathered at one end, standing around a high wire fence that surrounded something I couldn't see from here.

Dad and Allie got out of the car, and I followed after them. As we neared the fence, I realized it enclosed a low pit—there was a gradual slope downward to a mass of leafy vegetation. Derek Bell came hurrying over, looking even twitchier than he had this morning.

"Are the victims in there?" Dad asked, nodding to the fence.

"Yeah. It's the access point to an old stormwater drain. A passerby spotted one of the bodies." Bell blinked in a stunned kind of way, like he couldn't quite absorb what had happened. "The victims . . . It's Tom Cavanagh and Martin Flint."

I gaped. "The director *and* the nurse are dead? Here? But then who died in the fire?"

"You're certain?" Dad asked.

"I know them both. There's no doubt." Bell dragged a trembling hand through his hair. "Killed with single stab wounds to the chest, probably sometime during the night."

"Anyone hear anything? See anything?"

"We don't know yet. No one's come forward, but it'll take a while to interview all the residents."

Bell nodded over at where a crowd of anxious people were clustered around a police officer. They were all speaking at once, pelting questions at the cop.

"But *who* died?"

"What happened to them?"

"Are we safe here?"

Bell looked pleadingly at Allie. "You think you could . . . ?"

She nodded and strode over, holding up her hands and speaking in a low, reassuring tone. Within a few minutes, the hubbub of voices had quieted.

"She's good with people, huh?" Dad asked.

But Bell's attention wasn't on Allie. Instead, he was looking around the street. "Why dump the bodies here, of all places . . . ?" He cast an uneasy glance back at the entrance to the drain.

"They weren't killed in there?" Dad asked.

"No. There's not enough blood. They had to have been killed somewhere else. I'm hoping someone heard a car, at least—I'm thinking the killer would've had to drive the bodies up to the drain, then carry them in . . . Anyway, come and see."

Dad followed Bell toward the gate in the fence, but not before shooting me a stern look that meant: *you are not to view homicide victims*. That was fine by me. I didn't want to look at murdered people and talk about how they'd died, any more than I wanted to think about the details of how *I'd* died. I'd leave that part of detecting to Dad.

I suddenly remembered how Catching had thought I was still here because someone had murdered me and I had "unfinished business." Could the ghosts of Cavanagh and Flint be about, clinging to their earthly remains? Although I hadn't stuck with my body. There'd been a period of nothingness, followed by drifting through colors—and then I'd heard Dad crying. When I reached him, I found that a couple of weeks had passed since the accident and my body was already buried.

The director and the nurse might be different to me, though. Except some deeper part of me was certain that they weren't around. I wasn't sure how I knew it, but I did. For whatever reason, there wasn't any unfinished business for them. I guessed it was up to Dad and me to figure out who had killed them, and why.

I turned my attention back to the residents. They were mostly people Dad's age or older. While there were no children outside, it was obvious by the toys scattered across the front gardens that families lived here. I hoped the kids weren't too scared.

I hoped Dad and I could solve this before anyone else got hurt.

Dad came back through the gate and strode away from the rest of the police, pulling out his phone to make a call. I went over to him and caught the end of a low-voiced conversation: "Yeah, quick as you can . . . There's definitely something off . . . I'll check in again later."

"Something off about what?" I demanded as he hung up.

He put his phone back to his ear so he could talk to me without getting stared at. "The case. Rachel's sending a team from the city; they should be here early tomorrow. I need some officers here who don't report to Derek Bell."

"He's scared, huh? After you left the station this morning, he was standing in the doorway, looking around like he thought someone might be after him."

Dad nodded, like he wasn't surprised. "That's how he looks now. I don't know how deep he's into whatever this is, but three people murdered in a town this size? Something's going on around here, and Bell knows more than he's saying."

Dad was right—the deaths couldn't possibly be unrelated. "This has to all be connected to the home, right? Wouldn't the kids who were in there know something?"

"Maybe." His mouth tightened. "But Rachel said they still aren't saying much. They could be scared. Kids like that, caught up in the system—it wouldn't have been hard for the men running the home to intimidate them into silence over a drugs operation. Or whatever was going on at that place."

"Director Cavanagh and Nurse Flint can't push them around now. Rachel should tell the kids that!"

"She'll do her best to reassure them, but . . ." He sighed. "Those kids have probably been failed so many times, they won't believe anyone in authority will treat them fairly. Besides, Rachel thinks there might be something else going on. She says it seems like they're *not* afraid, almost like they think everything's been taken care of. I suppose they might just want to put the home behind them. It's gone now, after all."

I thought back to the not-quite-smiling faces of the kids in the photo Dad had shown me. The home was supposed to have been a place that was good for them. It might've been too, if Allie and the other people who'd wanted to volunteer had been allowed in. Instead, they'd been shut out, so that Sholt could sell drugs or whatever he'd been doing. And Derek Bell hadn't done anything about it either because he was involved or because the Sholts were rich and powerful. "How those kids were treated—it's not right!"

I sounded like Dad. He heard it too; his mouth curved into a smile. "No, it isn't. But the boss is onto it. She'll find a way to get the kids to trust her, and get them all the help she can too. She's got the city end of this. I need to work things here."

I could help him with that. "Well, if Cavanagh *was* at the Sholt place, maybe Flint was there too, hiding out from the cops. Last night, there was some kind of fight—which is how the window got smashed—and Alexander Sholt killed them both. Then he dumped the bodies here because . . . um . . ."

"It might have just been the first place that came to mind," Dad said. "Everyone around here seems to have known about the old drain. But there's something else." He nodded toward the fence. "See the gate? It was locked. The police had to use bolt cutters to get in, and there's no sign of any tampering."

"Then how did Sholt—or whoever it was—get the bodies in there?" I asked.

"I don't know! It's like they fell out of the sky. But they couldn't have, of course." He shrugged. "Someone probably tampered with the lock in a way that isn't immediately apparent. Except that means someone went to all the trouble of concealing the break-in, only to leave the bodies where they could be easily spotted. Although, I suppose it's possible that Sholt thought the bodies were better hidden than they were, especially since they seem to have been dumped here last night. It would've been dark—he would've been panicked . . ."

He fell into silence, frowning his thinking frown.

After a moment, his gaze sharpened, focusing on something past me, and he put the phone back in his pocket. I turned to see Allie approaching.

As she neared us, Dad asked, "Did you know the victims well?"

"Not at all, really. Just to say hello to. Those two kept themselves to themselves." She shifted to look toward the drain and then past it, staring at . . . a bus stop?

"It's so strange," Allie murmured. "We were only talking about Sarah this morning."

"What's the connection?" Dad asked.

"This is the last place she was seen," Allie replied. "She got off the school bus there, and she would've walked right down this street to get to her house, which was a block away. She vanished somewhere between here and her home."

"Maybe it's all linked somehow!" I exclaimed. Then I thought about it. "Except . . . Tom Cavanagh and Martin Flint couldn't possibly have known Sarah. They weren't from around here. So probably not."

Allie had reached the same conclusion. "There's no real connection, of course. Just coincidence."

Dad nodded his agreement. "Did any of the residents see or hear anything?"

She shook her head. "We'll need to conduct proper interviews, but no one's volunteering any information." Her face lightened. "Well, except for Tansy Webster and her angels."

"Angels?"

Allie nodded at the crowd. "See the woman in green?"

There were several women wearing green, and I was trying to figure out which one she was talking about when Allie added, "With the dogs?"

Oh, *that* woman: the old lady in the tracksuit with four fluffy white mutts sitting at her feet.

Dad nodded, and Allie continued, "That's Tansy. She's a big believer in . . . well, lots of things. Anyway, she's insisting she heard wings beating in the air above her house last night, only they sounded too large to belong to a bird. The dogs heard it too, she said; barked half the night."

Wings in the air. Too large for a bird.

My heart slammed against the walls of my chest.

"Dad. *Fetchers!*"

My father gave a slight shake of his head.

"I don't care whether you believe Catching or not," I told him. "*I* do. The Fetchers could be looking for her, and I'm going to see if she's okay!"

I ran, so worried for Catching that I was streets away from Dad before it dawned on me that I didn't know how to get to the hospital from here. But I could always get to Dad by focusing on him. Maybe it would work the same way with her?

I closed my eyes, picturing Isobel Catching's sharp-edged face in my mind. After a second, I began to have a sense of her. It was faint at first and difficult to pin down, almost like she was moving, but then it grew steady and strong. I concentrated. Everything shifted around me, as if the entire world was a deck of cards that was shuffling itself into a different order. When I felt it all settle back into place, I opened my eyes again.

I was standing at the end of Catching's hospital bed. Words rushed out of me: "Catching, there might be Fetchers around—Fetchers who've come into this world. Some people have died—"

"I heard. It's all the nurses can talk about."

"—and there was a witness who heard wings beating in the air, too big for a bird, and I think they might be coming for you."

Catching held up a hand. "Slow down, Teller. It's not Fetchers."

"Are you sure?"

"Yep."

"Are you really—" I substituted a more useful question: "*How* can you be sure?"

"No one's coming to get me. Promise."

She sounded absolutely positive. Maybe Dad was right and there weren't such things as Fetchers. And yet I couldn't shake the feeling that there was truth in Catching's story. Either way, I felt dizzy with relief now that the threat was gone—or, okay, it seemed the threat had never actually existed, at least not in this dimension. But I'd thought it had.

Catching pointed to the end of the bed. "You'd better sit before you fall." I sat, and she added, "Thanks anyway. For coming to help me."

"Yeah, well. It's what fr—" I caught myself on the word. Catching wouldn't want to be called my friend.

But to my astonishment, she said, "Guess it is what friends do."

"Um. Are we friends, then?"

She regarded me with an expression that said I'd failed to understand something. "I told you what I thought about your dad, didn't I?"

I wasn't sure what that had to do with anything. "Yeah."

"So we're friends. Because friends always tell each other the truth. Even when it hurts."

That was a very . . . Catching definition of friendship.

But I'd take it. I grinned at her. She didn't exactly return the smile, but one corner of her mouth pulled up. *Close enough.*

She shook her head at me, still with the almost-smile lingering on her lips. "You're an idiot! If there were Fetchers here, what were you gonna do? *Haunt* them?"

"I don't know! I probably should've waited for my dad. I'm pretty sure he'll follow me here, by the way. Oh, and I haven't told him that you can see me. I didn't want . . . that is, I . . ."

"You didn't want me telling him he's sad? I think he already knows."

"I don't want you reminding him!"

"Relax, Teller. I won't tell him I can see you."

"Really?"

"Really. I told you what I think, because that's what friends do. Now I'll keep your secret. That's what friends do too."

I wondered if Catching had a list of rules written down somewhere of how to be friends. I'd never met anyone like her. I didn't think there *was* anyone like her. "Thanks."

She nodded, her gaze turning inward. "I had a friend. In the beneath-place. She used to tell me true things. Or true as she saw it."

"Things that hurt?"

Catching's almost-smile vanished and her hand clenched into a fist, bunching up the sheet where she was gripping it. I'd spoken without thinking, and I felt terrible. Her friend *had* told her things that hurt.

I was more convinced than ever that Catching had been through something awful—and apparently she hadn't been alone. But her friend wasn't here now, and the fact that Catching hadn't mentioned her before made me worry about her fate . . . and about whether Catching herself was still in danger, whatever she said.

"I know you haven't exactly seen my dad at his best," I told her, "but he's the person I'd call if I was in trouble. He can help you. You just have to give him a chance."

"I'm not telling you what happened to ask for help," she said.

"Then why are you telling it?"

Catching drew her legs up to her chest and rested her chin on her knees. "To be heard."

I was silent for a moment, thinking about that. Then I said, "Well, that kind of sounds like asking for help. And even if it isn't, just because you're not asking doesn't mean you don't need it."

Catching said nothing; she just watched me out of those fathomless brown eyes. But it wasn't uncomfortable sitting here together. In fact, it was nice to sit quietly with someone out of choice, instead of doing it because they didn't know I was there. It had been nice to have a normal conversation too. Well, okay, not *totally* normal—but Catching telling me I was an idiot was an ordinary thing for one friend to say to another.

I suddenly found myself missing the cousins. They were the ones who usually teased me over my mistakes. And they defended me, if anyone outside the family dared to laugh at even the stupidest things I did. Like the time I'd thought I could sing. I'd been ten years old and halfway through my big performance at the school assembly when I'd realized the teachers were wincing and the kids were clapping their hands over their ears. It had been such a shock; Aunty Viv had always said I had a lovely voice! It wasn't until the horrible moment on the stage that I'd remembered she'd said the salt cake was lovely too. I'd stuttered into silence. Kids had begun to giggle, and I'd almost burst into tears. Then the cousins had started shouting.

First Dennis: *Shut up and let her sing!*

Then Trisha: *Like any of you could do as good!*

Angie: *None of you are better than her!*

And finally six-year-old Charlie: *None of you are better than* any *of us!*

Catching and I sat in a comfortable silence that was broken only by footsteps in the hall outside. I recognized my father's brisk tread and stood up just as he came bursting through the door.

"Hi, Dad. No Fetchers after all. Sorry."

He shot me a look that said *I told you so.* But he couldn't have been sure, or he wouldn't have come charging in like that. Dad wasn't completely convinced he was right about Catching making everything up, no matter what he claimed.

"Come to hear the rest of the story, policeman?" Catching asked.

"I suppose I have," Dad answered. "If you want to tell it."

I remembered he'd said he wanted to talk to Catching again, back when we discovered that the person who died at the home had been stabbed. It seemed like we'd found that out a thousand years ago. It had only been this morning.

Dad pulled a chair away from the wall, placing it beside the bed and sitting down. "Would you like to tell me about the fire this time?"

She sniffed. "We haven't got to that part yet. And the next part . . ." Her gaze drifted to me for a moment and then away again before Dad could realize she was seeing me. "The next part is about my friend. And the gray."

Catching

THE PRISONER

I wake.
There's a light above.
It shines on the center of the room. Leaves shadows at the
edges.
A voice speaks: "Hello, girl."

I sit up. "Who's there?"
"Me is here."

I turn toward the sound.
Corner of the room.
Too dark to see into.

The voice sings:
"One more for the Feed.
Dead girl, dead girl.
One more in need.
Dead girl, dead girl.
Cry yourself to sleep.

Dead girl, dead girl.
Today monsters eat.
Dead girl, dead girl."

I jump off the bed. Put up my fists. "Come out!"
No answer.
I take a step. Stop.
I don't know who's in that corner. *What's* in that corner.
"Who are you?" I ask.
"Who are *you*? A name for a name!"
One of us has to go first. "I'm Isobel Catching."
"I'm Crow."
"Come out where I can see you, Crow."
"You'll be afraid if I do."
I snort. "Yeah. 'Cause singing creepy songs in the dark isn't
scary at all."

I hear shuffling.
Someone appears.
She's gray.
Gray skin. Gray hair that trails to the floor.
Gray dress *made* from her hair.
She watches me with clouded eyes.
"Are you afraid, Isobel-the-Catching?"
No. Relieved. I drop my fists. "You're a girl. Like me."

She comes—*hops*—closer. Her feet turn inward. Her nails
are too long.

"*Not* like you!" she says. "You have colors. So many. Soon they'll come, and you won't be full of colors. You'll be full of screams."

"Who's coming? The Fetchers?"

"Fetchers!" she sniffs. "They are nothing. No heart, no guts, no core. Here, they serve the Feed."

The boss man. "What does he want with us?"

"He eats what's inside our *insides*. The colors that live in our spirits. Do you think I was always a gray girl?"

Colors are not for Fetchers!
The colors are for him.
I *had* thought Crow was a gray girl.
But Crow's colors have been taken.
All her colors.

"How long have you been here?"

Crow hops about. "Since the Feed began. I wait. I watch. I help those who come."

"Yeah? Help me, then!"

"I *am* helping. I am telling."

"Tell me how we get out."

Crow slashes her fingernails through the air.

"There's no *escape*. Not unless you're a dead girl."

Her head snaps around to the door.
It rattles.
She shuffles back to her dark corner.

The door opens.

First and Second are here.

Second throws something at me. I snatch it out of the air.

A bread roll.

I'm hungry.

But there's only one.

I look at Crow's corner.

She's gone quiet.

She doesn't want it.

Or she's hiding.

As if they don't know you're here, Crow.

I tear the bun in two.

Throw her half on my bed.

Eat the other.

She speaks from the dark: "Sometimes bread. Sometimes meat. Sometimes *sleep*."

My legs go numb.

I fall.

The Fetchers carry me out of the room.

Crow's voice follows:

"One more for the Feed.

Dead girl, dead girl . . ."

THE FEED

I'm taken through tunnels.
To a room.
Dropped on the floor.
Like luggage.
The Fetchers leave.
I stay.

There's a table in front of me.
It's made of gray branches.
The branches rise up into thin sticks.
The sticks curl open like fingers.
On the other side of it, in the darkness, something moves.

I get up. Fight. Escape.
Only I don't. I can't move.
Not my fingers.
Nor my toes.
I can only feel.
Only look.

The thing comes out of the shadows.
The Feed is large. White. Thin.
He has legs like broomsticks and arms that reach to his
feet.
He bends to inspect me.
His eyes are mirrors.
I can see my frozen face.
I look terrified.

I *am* terrified.

The Feed grabs my wrist.
Drags me across the room.
My head is clutched.
Long fingers dig into my skull.
He lifts me off the ground.
I want to snarl.
Yell.
Bite.
But I can't.

My body is placed onto the table.
The Feed brings his face centimeters from my own.
His breath is on my cheek.
His mirror eyes peer into my brain.
He keeps his gaze on mine. Rears back.
Pushes aside the clothes covering my stomach.
His fingers press below my belly button.

My flesh tears in two.

I scream.

Only my mouth doesn't work.

He holds up his hand. Colors drip from his fingers.

As if I'm bleeding rainbows.

He eats what's inside *our insides.*

The Feed swallows down a strip of green.

A faint glow fills his skin. Fades away.

He peels away another piece of me.

Then another.

My eyes leak hot tears.

My throat rips itself apart with screams I can't scream.

The pain's going to kill me.

It doesn't.

I live.

I feel.

I hurt.

THE GRAY

I'm a ball curled up.
I'm a glass thrown against rock.
Shattered. Bits of me everywhere.
I'll never find them all.
No one will.

Crow whispers in my ear: "If you are a dead girl, you won't
feel. You won't hurt."
I turn my head into my pillow.
Say nothing.

"Are you angry, Isobel-the-Catching? About the bread?"
She waits.
I keep saying nothing.
"If you don't eat, they make you. Sometimes bread,
sometimes meat. Sometimes sleep—but not always. Only
when they want you for the Feed."
She waits more. I'm still silent.

Crow stamps her foot. Long nails rake the ground.
"What could I do? What can you do? Fetchers are never

caught. They are never stopped. We have no claws or wings or bite. We can't get away. *No* one gets away."
No one gets away . . . ?

I push words through my hurt throat. "There are other girls?"
"The Fetchers fetch. The Feed is fed. The girls come but never go."
Crow's voice is heavy. Sad.
The other girls are dead.
That's not going to be me.

I sit up. "I'm getting out."
"I know how."
"Tell me, then!"
"You must become a dead girl. A not-feeling girl."
Dead inside? Stupid idea.
I slam my hand on the bed.
"Tell me how to really escape!"
"That is how! And you must be dead *soon*. Then you won't mind being a gray girl."
I stand. Glare. "I'm not going to be gray, Crow!"
Her mouth turns down. "Foolish not-a-dead girl." She points to my arm. "You already are."

I look at where she points.
There are finger marks on my wrist. Where the Feed first touched me.
The marks are *gray.*

I scratch.

Dig.

But I can't claw the horrible from myself.

I can't make the color come back.

"It doesn't come off," Crow says. "It is your gray. Like mine, but not. Everyone's gray is their own."

She leans closer and adds, "You wouldn't mind so much if you were a dead girl."

"Get away from me!" I snap.

Crow jumps back. "Fine! Put all your screams upon your shoulders and let them *crush* you."

She hops into her corner.

I stare at my hand.

I want a knife. To cut it out of me.

That's dumb.

If I get a knife, I'll use it on the Feed.

The Feed took from me.

Left his mark on me.

Everyone can see it.

I don't know how to stand this.

Only I do know.

The names.

Granny Trudy Catching . . .

Nanna Sadie Catching . . .

Grandma . . . Linda?
I can't remember.

I'm glass thrown against rock.
My connections are broken.
I grab hold of bits of myself.
Push pieces back together.

Granny Trudy Catching . . .
Nanna Sadie Catching . . .
Grandma Leslie Catching . . .

Grandma Leslie Catching.
My mother's mother.
Mum's voice speaks:

The law that let the government take Aboriginal children
lasted for generations. They came for your Grandma when
she was a kid, just as they'd come for her mum before her. But
your Grandma didn't get away.

They put her in a bad place. One of the worst places. She
thought her mum would save her. Until an older kid told
her how it was. The mothers weren't told where their kids
had been taken to. And the government never gave anyone
back. That was when your Grandma knew she'd have to live
through hard day after hard day. She worried she couldn't do
it. That she wasn't tough enough. Then she remembered the

111

rocks of her homeland. Old rocks. Rocks that had lived for
millions of years.

Your Grandma made herself strong like rock. She survived
hard times. She survived hard years. She got through until she
was grown up. Then she went looking for her mum, who'd
never stopped looking for her.

Your Grandmother knew how to endure.

I'm not glass thrown against rock.
I *am* the rock.
I can endure.
As long as I remember where I come from.
Who I come from.

Crow can help me with that.
I can't tell her the names out loud.
But I don't have to.
Just who they are to me.

"Crow? I need you to do something."
Silence.
"I need you to say some names with me."
More silence.
"Come out and help!"
"I *did* help."

She's sulking.
Because I didn't like her twisted idea.
She's messed up. But I need her.
"Crow? I'll think about being a dead, not-feeling girl."
She bounces out of the shadows. "Really?"
No. "Yes. So long as you learn some words."
"I am good at words!"

I say the names.
She repeats them.
We say them together.
"Granny . . ." *Trudy Catching.*
"Nanna . . ." *Sadie Catching.*
"Grandma . . ." *Leslie Catching.*
"Mum . . ." *Rhonda Catching.*
"Me."

Even if I forget again, Crow will remember.
I'll endure.
Until I get away.
Until the Feed knows fear.
That fear will wear my face.
Speak with my voice.

And I'll be terrifying.

Beth

THE COLORS

Catching went silent.

Dad didn't say anything. I didn't say anything. No words would come out of my mouth. I was too shocked. Too horrified. Too enraged.

My father was angry too. I could see it in the tightness around his mouth and the glint in his eyes. But his voice was gentle when he spoke to Catching: "If someone has harmed you, I can protect you. I can protect your friend."

"Trying to save me?" Her face was stony and remote. *Like the rock that endures.* "Too late."

Dad tried again. "If your friend is in trouble . . ."

"She's not."

That had the ring of truth to it. But I was convinced now that everything Catching said was true in some way.

Dad took his card out of his pocket, placing it on the nightstand beside the bed. "This is my number. You can call me anytime."

"Yeah, I'll *so* be doing that."

He sighed. "Are you sure there's nothing else you'd like to tell me?"

Catching flopped back against her pillows and closed her eyes. Dad took the hint. "I'll let you rest." He rose to his feet. "I'll be here tomorrow, and we can talk again, if you'd like."

He walked out of the room with slow steps, giving her the chance to call him back. But she didn't speak or move until the door swung closed behind him. Then her eyes flicked open and she sat up.

I wanted to say . . . I didn't know, something, although everything I could think of seemed shallow and stupid next to the awfulness of her experience. I spoke anyway. "I know you don't want Dad's help, but if *I* can do anything . . ."

She gave an impatient shake of her head. "You want to help somebody, Teller? Try yourself."

"I'm fine!"

"You're *so* not. You don't want to move on to what's next? Fine. Be stupid, and don't. But you can't go back. Your dad can't either."

He can! I can! But those words sounded ridiculous even inside my own head. I'd died. I was different. Dad was different. I couldn't reverse that.

I don't know why I hadn't known it until this instant.

Catching studied my face, and whatever she saw in my expression made the half-smile return to her mouth. She lay back, apparently feeling she'd made her point. "Get out of here. I'll see you tomorrow."

I left, drifting out of the hospital into the darkening light of the late afternoon. My father was pacing back and forth by the car, talking on his phone. He hung up just as I reached him.

"Break in the case?" I asked.

"No, just getting someone to take a look at that rehab facility Catching was in." He cast a worried glance back at the hospital. "I think someone really hurt her. Maybe at that facility. Or maybe before then. It's hard to tell, with the way she's mixing everything together." He sighed. "Unfortunately, there are limits to what I can do if she won't give me more to go on."

"I think the story might be all you get, Dad."

Because Catching didn't want to be helped. Only heard. And while I hadn't believed that at first, I was starting to. She obviously thought she could look after herself. And I supposed it was no surprise she didn't want to rely on anyone else, when there'd been no one to come the time she'd needed it most.

Dad's phone rang. He pulled it back out and looked down at the name of the caller. Aunty Viv.

I rolled my eyes as he shoved the phone into his pocket. "You're not going to be able to ignore her forever. Grandpa Jim's birthday is coming up, you know." Mum's dad was going to be eighty-two in a month. "What are you going to do, avoid Aunty Viv for the entire party? Because that will be weird."

"I'm probably not going," Dad said.

Just like that. As if it was nothing.

"What do you mean, you're not going? You have to go!"

"No. I don't."

"Of course you do, y—"

"Leave it, Beth!" he snarled.

I took a startled step back. Dad's gaze dropped to the ground. He shifted uncomfortably and mumbled, "Sorry. Um. Guess we should be getting back to the hotel."

He went to the car and opened the passenger-side door. It was a thing he did sometimes, opening doors for me as if I couldn't phase right through them. It usually happened when he most wanted to pretend I was still alive. I was supposed to let him pretend, the way I always did. That meant getting into the car and shutting up about Aunty Viv.

I flashed back to being outside this hospital with Dad yesterday. The only thing I'd cared about then was him not being sad. I would have let go of Grandpa Jim's birthday, thinking I could always talk to him about it another time.

Yesterday was a different world.

Today I did something I'd never done before.

I walked away.

Dad called after me. But I sped up, running back to the hospital and right through its walls, then through building after building in the streets behind. When I felt sure Dad wouldn't be able to find me, I shifted onto the footpath and slowed to a stroll, going nowhere in particular except away from my father.

I couldn't believe Dad. This was *Grandpa Jim*. My Grandfather with the big white hair. The man who'd taught me card tricks, and who hadn't spoken a single word for a full three days after I'd died. The parent who'd always treated Dad like one of his own sons.

It had never occurred to me that Dad wouldn't go to

Grandpa Jim's birthday party. Aside from anything else, it was the first family birthday since my death. Everyone would be sad and happy at the same time—or at least *trying* to be happy. And they'd all expect Dad to be there.

I could just see Aunty Viv, her eyes darting constantly to the front door as she waited for Dad to walk through it. When she finally realized he wasn't coming . . . when they all realized he wasn't coming . . . I knew exactly how it would be.

Aunty Viv would deflate like a balloon with all the air let out of it. Aunty June would stomp around, muttering under her breath. Uncle Mick and his husband would try to cheer Grandpa Jim up with a card game, but Grandpa wouldn't really be having fun, no matter how many times they let him win at rummy. And Uncle Kel and his wife would go cook something. But not even Kel's best stew or Marie's most chocolatey pudding would comfort the cousins, who'd go quiet the way they only ever did when something was really wrong. It would be awful, and I wasn't sure Dad would ever be able to make up for it.

There was a queasy sensation in my stomach. Had I been getting things wrong, all this time? I'd been focused on getting Dad back to who he'd been before I died. Now I was thinking I should have been helping him go *on* to become a person who knew how to live in a world where I wasn't alive. A person who'd go to Grandpa Jim's birthday.

I had no idea what to do anymore.

I also didn't know when it had become night.

I stopped, puzzled; I hadn't noticed the light changing. Then I realized I could see twilight in the distance. It *wasn't* night. But I was enveloped by a huge shadow with curving shapes at the edges. As if some big, clawed thing loomed at my back . . .

I spun around, heart pounding. There was nothing there.

Maybe the shadow *was* the big, clawed thing.

And I was inside of it.

I sprinted for the twilight, reached it, and kept going. But the shadow followed, streaming over the earth to flow at my heels. I ran faster. The shadow flowed faster. I pulled every last scrap of speed from my body, my arms and legs pumping until my chest was tight and my limbs were trembling. I couldn't keep this up! And the shadow was still coming.

Maybe I could escape it by reshuffling the world. I tried focusing on Dad. But my mind couldn't seem to grab on to him. I tried thinking of Catching instead. That didn't work either, and my legs were rubbery and weak and slowing down. The thing was almost upon me, and I'd reached the limits of my body's endurance.

Except that I didn't have an actual body. I was dead.

With that realization, I burst through limits that weren't there anymore and ran as I'd never been able to before. The shakiness in my arms and legs vanished. The pain in my chest vanished. Only the joy of motion remained—my hair whipping back from my face, the thud of my feet on the earth, the cool sting of the wind on my skin. I was faster than the shadow. I was faster than anyone or anything. I'd never felt more . . . *alive.*

Something shining flashed into existence in front of me.

I skidded to a halt, casting a glance back over my shoulder. But the shadow was gone. There was only what lay ahead: a sea of colors brighter than any I'd ever seen. I took a curious step forward. The shining, writhing coils were a strange sight, and yet I wasn't afraid. Somehow, I knew these colors; more than knew them—loved them and had missed them, although I hadn't known it until right now. A fierce longing overtook me. I wanted to go home.

I bounded forward. Then I realized what I was seeing and feeling, and stopped.

At least, my brain decided to stop. But my legs kept on moving, carrying me to where my heart wanted to go.

I focused my will and staggered to a slow and reluctant halt.

The colors were the place I'd glimpsed right after I'd died. The other side. And they were singing, or someone was. I couldn't make out the words, but it sounded like a welcoming song. The kind a mother might sing to her child.

I'd finally found Mum. Except she'd been with me all along, because I *knew* the sound of her voice. I'd heard it a thousand times, only I'd thought it was my own voice. She was the part of me that said *Everything will be all right,* and *You did great at that,* and *It's going to be an amazing day.* Mum had been there my whole life, helping me be a butterfly girl.

Maybe all hopeful thoughts were just someone who loved

123

us, reaching out from another side. Which meant I could be there for my family even after I'd crossed over!

Joy bubbled up in me and I leaped forward, rising into the air. Then I thought of my father and fell back to earth.

I couldn't go. Because while the rest of the family could have a relationship with who I was now, Dad could only manage one with who I'd been before. He needed me to be here in the same way as I had been when I was alive, or as much like it as was possible.

I took one last, long look at the colors, and sucked in a steadying breath.

Then I turned my back.

There was a popping sound. The whole world turned dull. The colors were gone. I fell to my knees, sobbing into the skirt of the stupid yellow dress I'd wear forever.

I sat there until my tears ran out and the world grew dark. It was really night this time. The shadow hadn't come back. Maybe it had been my own death, chasing me to where I was supposed to go. I didn't know, and I didn't have the strength to care. Turning away from the colors had taken everything I had.

I lurched up. It seemed to take a lot of effort. *Maybe I should sit again?* Except I was already on my feet. I took a step, another step, a third. Now it seemed easier to keep on walking than not, so I kept going, making my way to the hotel.

The light was on in Dad's room, shining through a crack in the curtains; he was still awake. Unless he'd fallen asleep with the lamp on again, but it seemed too early in the evening for that. I squared my shoulders, bracing myself to find him crying, and walked into the room.

He wasn't crying. He was sitting in a chair with his back to me, staring at a wall filled with sticky notes grouped under three headings: ISOBEL CATCHING, SARAH BLUE, and THE HOME.

I blinked in surprise. "Dad, you made one of your thinking walls?"

"Beth!" He leaped up. "You're back! I didn't know when— You've been crying."

My eyes felt red and gritty. *Stupid, Beth.* I was usually so careful to make sure he never knew I cried.

"I'm sorry," Dad rushed on, "so sorry I snapped at you. I didn't mean to; I just . . . I'm sorry."

I wanted to tell him I hadn't been crying because of that. Except I didn't want to talk about the colors. "S'okay."

Dad didn't seem to know what to say, and I couldn't find any more words either. Finally he waved at the wall. "I've been mapping everything out. Seeing if anything connects."

He paused in a hopeful kind of way.

You want us to be friends again, Dad? Promise to go to Grandpa Jim's birthday.

But he was trying, and I was too worn out to fight. "You think it *is* all connected?" I asked.

Dad's face lightened; he was relieved to have gotten a response out of me. "I don't know. Maybe. Except I can't see a link between Sarah and everything else." He cast a frustrated glance back at the wall. "About the only thing I'm sure of is that I need to confirm whether anyone has actually seen or spoken to Alexander Sholt since the fire."

"His dad saw him," I pointed out wearily. "He said Sholt left for the city this morning, remember?"

"Someone else."

I didn't see why that would be important— Wait. Suddenly I wasn't so tired. "You think it might have been *Sholt* who died in the fire? But why would his father lie?"

"Family pride? He could be trying to buy time for Derek Bell to cover up whatever Alexander was involved in. Or he could be moving his son's money around, hiding funds he doesn't want uncovered in a police investigation into Alexander's murder."

That made sense. Not much else did. "If Alexander Sholt died first, who killed everybody else? *Bell?*"

"Possibly, but . . ." Dad shook his head. "I can't see it. He seemed genuinely shocked this morning when those bodies were found."

He turned back to the wall, frowning. I walked over to stand with him. The pieces of this case had just been flung up into the air, and I was struggling to put them into an order that formed a coherent picture.

I knew this was a victory, of sorts—Dad was properly back to work. A few days ago, I would have been jumping for joy. Now I wanted more. I wanted him to talk to Aunty Viv. I wanted him to go to Grandpa Jim's party. I wanted him to reconnect with the world. Because then I could . . .

I turned my face away from Dad.

Then I could go.

I loved my father. But I knew something that I hadn't known before—at least, not all the way to my bones, the way I knew it now.

I didn't belong here anymore.

THE COP

It was morning and I was standing by the window, watching Dad take the sticky notes off the wall to keep them from the prying eyes of whoever cleaned the rooms. We'd sat up half the night poring over those notes and gotten nowhere. Then Dad had fallen asleep and I'd paced the room, thinking. Only not about the case.

I was trapped between two different sides to the world, and not truly a part of either one. But there was no changing that unless I could change Dad. I had to help him become the Michael Teller who could accept who I was now. And if he never did become that person, I guessed I was here forever. But I wasn't going to think about what years upon years of this dreary half-existence would be like. I wasn't thinking about anything that weighed me down. I still wanted to be a butterfly girl, even if I couldn't fly away.

Dad was taking a long time with those notes. If he didn't speed up, he'd be late to meet up with the city cops, who'd arrived early this morning. He just didn't seem able to remove the last note, the one that said SARAH BLUE. He kept reaching for it and then letting his hand fall.

"Did you figure out a connection between Sarah and everything else?" I asked.

"No." He finally took the note down. But he didn't tuck it away in his suitcase with the others. Instead, he stood with it cupped in his hand, holding the paper as if it was something fragile and precious.

"It wasn't done right," he said softly. "The investigation, after she disappeared. That file . . ." He shook his head. "There are things you do when a kid goes missing, and none of them were done. Someone should have noticed."

"It's no big surprise that Derek Bell's dad didn't get called out for sloppy work," I said. "He was the boss cop back then."

"That wasn't why no one noticed," Dad replied. "Or not the only reason. If a white girl had gone missing like that, just vanished on her way home from school"—he shook his head in disgust—"there'd have been an outcry. It would have been on the news, in the papers, something everyone talked about on the street. Instead, the only people speaking for Sarah— her family, her friend—were ignored." His mouth twisted. "Gerry Bell got away with not doing enough because people didn't care enough. No one was paying attention."

And Dad took that personally. He pretty much took all injustice personally, but especially anything to do with Aboriginal people not being treated right. And as he'd told me a thousand times over, growing up in his father's town had taught him that one person in power could do bad things, but it took lots of people to let the bad things continue.

Dad didn't want to be one of the people who didn't pay attention. He didn't want to be anything like his father either.

I'd always wanted to be exactly like mine. Only I was Mum's daughter too. I knew how to leave behind the things that had to be left behind. And it suddenly dawned on me that Dad—who carried the weight of unjust things—might be holding on to something that wasn't his to bear.

"Dad? You do know that you couldn't have saved me, right?"

Dad bent to put the note away, placing it gently into his suitcase. Then he straightened up and spoke in a voice so low I had to edge forward to catch the words. "It was my job to keep you safe."

"You couldn't protect me from an accident! No one could."

He sniffed and wiped at his eyes. My father was crying. I wished I could hug him. But the only way I could reach him was with words.

"If you're not going to the birthday because you think anyone blames you . . ."

"That's not why," he answered huskily. "It's the cousins."

That made no sense. "But you love the cousins! *I* love the cousins!"

His gaze slid to the floor. "I know. That's why I shouldn't be around them."

"Why not?"

"Because I failed you!" He looked up at me, the tears rolling down his cheeks. "I couldn't keep you safe. I couldn't take care of *my* child. I don't deserve to go to birthday parties and watch the cousins grow up, when you'll never . . ."

I finished the sentence for him: "When I'll never grow up."

I finally understood. I even understood why he'd snarled at me back at the hospital car park: I'd jabbed at an open wound. I could see in his face how raw and bleeding this pain was for him.

Dad half sat, half fell onto the bed. I stayed on my feet, my head spinning. My father was impossibly turned around inside his own mind. I groped my way to more words—any words—that might make a difference, fumbling for a way to show him how far he was from being who he should be.

"Dad, you're . . . You know, I told Catching you were the person I'd call if I was in trouble. But now you're not . . . you can't . . ."

I was getting stupidly mixed up, and I had to do better. I tried again.

"You taught me to be fair, Dad, and what you're doing's not fair to anybody. Especially me. How do you think I'm going to feel if I'm the reason you make everybody miserable? And if you can't see how wrong you are—how *unfair* you're being, to yourself and everybody else—then you're not the dad I know."

I wasn't sure if I'd made sense to him. He was living in an upside-down world, believing upside-down things. But after a second, he whispered, "I'll try."

Did that mean he'd try to go to the birthday party? Or just try in general? I wasn't sure, and I didn't think he was either. But at least he understood that he needed to change. For now that was enough. It had to be, because it was obvious he wasn't up to talking about this anymore.

Dad lumbered to the bathroom and splashed cold water onto his face. Then he grabbed his car keys, and we headed to the station to meet the city cops.

I talked as we motored along—prattled, really, like Allie, but only about the case. I didn't say anything new, and neither did he, but that didn't matter. What mattered was for him to be able to have a conversation without his voice breaking or his eyes tearing up, and by the time we reached the station, he'd pushed his feelings far enough away to be able to do that.

I'd fully expected Derek Bell to get in Dad's way at every available opportunity, since he obviously wasn't going to be happy about the management of the case being transferred over to Dad and the city cops. But Bell wasn't even there. He was out with Allie, interviewing the people who lived on the street where the bodies had been found. That meant the handover of the case went pretty smoothly. It also meant it was all kind of boring.

I hung about, becoming increasingly restless as the morning wore on. Dad kept glancing at the door, waiting for Bell and Allie to return. Only, when Allie finally did arrive, she was alone. And she looked a little worried.

Dad strode over. "Derek not with you?"

"I was actually hoping he was here." She glanced about the station as if she was going to find him in a corner somewhere. "He called last night to say he wasn't feeling well, and said that if he didn't show up this morning, I should just do the interviews without him. So I did."

"Have you heard from him today?"

"No. I've tried calling, but he's not answering." She bit her lip. "Do you think . . . I mean, what if he's collapsed or something? He really didn't look well yesterday afternoon—he was sweating and shaky and so pale. I thought he might have food poisoning."

I snorted. "He was *scared*. On account of how the web of lies he's a part of is slowly unraveling. Maybe he's done a runner, Dad!"

Dad gave a small nod. To Allie, he said, "Tell you what, why don't we go out to Derek's place and check on him?"

"You think we should? He's never liked people dropping by, but I really am worried. I can go on my own, though—I'm sure you have other things to do."

"It's no problem," Dad replied. "I have a few things to confirm with him anyway. I'm assuming it won't take long to get to his house?"

Allie widened her eyes in mock outrage. "Are you trying to say this place is small? I'll have you know Derek lives on the *edge* of town." She grinned. "So, no, it won't take long to get there."

Derek Bell's house was a big old weatherboard a little out of town and well away from any neighbors. I looked around as I followed Allie and Dad up the front path, but there was nothing much to see: dust, trees, crows, sky. All of it quiet and still.

Dad pushed the doorbell. It chimed loud in the silence, but nobody answered.

133

Allie pulled out her phone. "I'll try calling again."

After a few seconds, there was a ringing from inside the house, faint but clear. Derek Bell's phone was in there somewhere. So where was he?

Dad frowned and went to the nearest window, cupping his hands around his eyes and peering through the glass. He shook his head in frustration. "There's something in the way. I can't get a clear view."

Allie darted over to the window on the other side of the door. "There's something blocking this one too. Wait, there's a gap! I can see—" She stepped back with a gasp. "He's on the floor! I think he's unconscious!"

Dad charged the front door. Once: it rattled on its hinges. Twice: it rattled some more. Dad put a hand to his shoulder and winced.

"You should stop before you really hurt yourself," I told him. But he just set his jaw and charged for a third time.

A gust of wind swept through, slamming against the wood along with my father. The door flew open. Dad's momentum carried him inside, and Allie dashed in after him. I waited a few moments before following, wanting to keep out of Dad's line of sight. I wasn't sure he'd want me going in . . . but he hadn't specifically told me to stay outside.

The door opened onto a gloomy hallway. I followed Dad's voice into the room Allie had looked into from the outside.

It was dark in here too. Big planks of wood had been nailed across all the windows, leaving only a few gaps for sunlight to filter through. In the dim light, I could make out shapes that told me I was in Derek Bell's living room: couch, bookcases, fireplace, knocked-over fire screen. Bell himself was lying on the floor, with Dad kneeling on one side of him and Allie on the other.

I edged closer to get a better view, and instantly wished I hadn't. There was a dark stain across Bell's chest. His eyes were open and staring.

He wasn't unconscious. He was dead.

I slapped a hand to my mouth to stifle a gasp and took a hasty step back.

"You should go back to the station," Dad said to Allie. "There's nothing you can do here."

I cast an uneasy glance around the room, not keen on encountering Derek's ghost—but he wasn't here. Things felt finished for him, just as they had for Nurse Flint and Director Cavanagh.

"I can handle this," Allie said. "I don't need to go back to the station."

"That's not what I meant," Dad replied. "This scene shouldn't be processed by people who worked for him. The city team can do it. And with Derek gone, you're the boss. This is going to be hard on the people who knew him."

"You don't just mean because he's dead, do you?" She cast a quick glance up at one of the boarded windows. "He was afraid of something, but he didn't ask for help. What was he involved in?"

"I'm not sure yet," Dad answered. "But yes, something's going on. There are going to be some tough days ahead."

Allie was quiet for a moment, absorbing that. Then she raised her head, like she was going to look whatever was coming right in the face, and rose to her feet to stride out of the house.

Dad stood as well, casting a searching glance around the room. Which was when he spotted me.

"Go outside, Beth! *Now.*"

I went. It was a relief to be back out in the fresh air and the sunshine. I hugged my arms around myself, shaky and shocked. I'd only seen Bell yesterday, weaselly but alive. Now he was gone. And based on the quick look I'd had at the body, I figured he'd been stabbed. Likely by the same person who'd murdered *three* other people.

And who might still be inside.

With my father.

I dashed back into the house. "*Dad!* The killer might still be here!"

He wasn't where I'd left him.

I darted through a doorway on the other side of the living room, blinking in the dimness. *Kitchen.* But Dad wasn't there either, or in the next room after that.

Then I heard his voice. I found him in a bedroom, talking on his phone: "Yes, like the others . . . I've sent Allison Hartley back to you. She can be trusted to manage the locals . . . See you when you get here."

"Dad, you could be in danger!" I shouted.

He hung up. "There's no one here but us, Beth."

"Are you sure?"

"I've looked around. And Bell's been dead for a while—he was likely killed last night."

"Oh." I put my hand to my heart, as if I could slow it down by pressing on it. Then I glared at Dad. "I couldn't find you. Why didn't you turn the lights on?"

"The electricity's out. I don't want you in here. Come on."

I followed him back through the gloom and out into the front garden. He strode all the way to the fence before he turned to study the house, frowning his thinking frown.

"There was no sign of forced entry before I knocked down the door," he mused. "And yet Bell was afraid."

I saw what he meant. "That means he must've let the killer in, yeah? Whoever it was walked right in the front door and out again afterward, closing it behind him? But there can't be that many people Bell trusts—so perhaps it *was* Sholt? Maybe he didn't die in the fire after all!"

"Maybe not. Bell was obviously terrified. And like you said, the only way in was—" Dad's mouth dropped open. He'd thought of something!

"What is it?"

"Nothing." But he was frowning deeper.

"Come on, Dad! I know you're thinking *something*."

He shook his head. "Nothing I'm sure of yet. I'll tell you when I am." He pulled out his phone and heaved a sigh. "Right now I have to call my boss and let her know we have another dead body—and this one's a cop."

I listened in as he talked to Rachel. I couldn't make out her words on the other end of the line, but she sounded

137

concerned, and I didn't think it was just because a police officer was dead. The straightforward case she'd given Dad to ease him back into work had turned into a quadruple homicide. I hoped the confidence in his voice would reassure her that he could cope. Dad was in control. Actually, I was pretty sure he was on the trail of something.

Cops from the city arrived while Dad was on the phone. He motioned them toward the house and hung up to follow them inside. Eventually Dad came back out, holding a set of car keys he must have borrowed from the city team.

"Are you going to tell me what you're thinking now?" I asked.

"Not yet," he replied. "First, there's someone we need to see."

THE STORY

I'd figured that we were headed for the Sholt house. But we went to the hospital.

"Catching's who you want to see?" I asked as Dad rolled the car to a stop. "You think she knows something that will help you solve Bell's murder?"

He didn't answer that. Instead, he said, "Before we go in, I need to ask you something. This morning, you said that you'd told Catching I was the person you'd call if you were in trouble. The thing is, Beth . . . how are you telling Catching anything?"

Oh. *Oh.* My stomach roiled. "Just because people can't hear you doesn't mean you can't tell them things."

Dad was watching me with a steady, patient expression. I hated that look. It was the one he used when he knew I was lying. "I think maybe she *can* hear you, Beth."

So he'd figured it out. I slumped in defeat, and his mouth quirked into a smile. "Why didn't you tell me?"

I looked down at my feet. "I don't know. I just didn't."

"That's not an answer."

I shrugged.

"Well," Dad said, "I suppose I could always ask Catching why you didn't—"

My head whipped up. "Don't do that!"

"If *you* tell me, I won't have to."

I couldn't have Catching saying to Dad that I was wasting my eternity trailing around after a sad old man. *Maybe she won't. Maybe she'll be nice to him because she's my friend.* But I couldn't be sure of that. For all I knew, Catching would think she was doing me a favor by telling Dad the truth as she saw it.

I had to find a way to say it that wasn't as harsh as how she'd put it.

"I . . . I didn't tell you because I didn't want you to talk to Catching about me," I said in a small voice. "She—well, she thinks I should move on."

He frowned. "*Is* there somewhere for you to move on to?"

I opened my mouth to say, *No. Of course not. There's only here.* Except the second I did it, the colors flashed into my mind and the words died in my throat. I couldn't bear to say that the colors weren't real.

I looked away from Dad, blinking back the traitor tears that had sprung into my eyes.

"Beth. Is there a place?"

I nodded. "It's full of colors."

"Is your mother there?"

I didn't answer that. He didn't ask again. Instead, he sat there in silence, watching me with that same steady regard. Waiting me out. "Yeah. She is."

Dad made a choked, hurt noise. I hurried to reassure him. "But I'm not going. I'm staying here. With you."

Except he didn't seem reassured. If anything, he seemed worried. "I never thought you were choosing to stay here! I thought this was just where you were. If there's a better place, a place with your mother, then isn't that somewhere you'd like to be?"

No. I like it here. But it was too big a lie to say, and it stuck in my throat.

Dad stared at me for a moment and then whispered, "You're staying because of me. Beth. I'll be okay."

I shook my head.

"I will, I promise you I—"

"You won't, Dad! You aren't. You're *sad.*"

Dad's face crumpled a little around the edges. And I didn't want to have this conversation anymore. I'd already decided I wasn't going to leave him until he was okay, and there was nothing he could say that would change my mind. It was just hurting us both to talk about it.

"I'm going inside to see Catching," I told him. "To talk about the *case.* Are you coming?"

"We can see Catching later! I think we should—"

I left the car, running right through the door and then the hospital walls until I reached Catching's room. I found her sitting on her bed, as always, and spoke in a rush: "Dad's coming, and he knows you can see me. I already told him what you think—about moving on, I mean—so you don't need to say anything to him about me leaving and him being a sad man, nothing at all!"

I'd just managed to get the last word out when Dad burst in. "Beth, we have to talk about this."

"We *really* don't."

Unexpectedly, Catching spoke: "No, you don't. Not now, anyway."

We both turned to look at her. *She's different.* Except she wasn't. It was the same old Catching, only . . . brighter? Her eyes seemed a little browner, her hair a little darker, and all her edges a little bit more pronounced.

"You didn't come here to fight with each other," Catching said. "You came for the story. You'll have to sit down, though. It's not a small ending."

We were *finally* going to find out about the fire? Dad had been right when he'd said we needed to see Catching, although I couldn't see how he'd known she would get to the end of her story today.

I settled onto the bed. Dad stayed where he was. "You may as well sit," I told him, "because I'm not talking about the other stuff, and if you keep trying to, I'll just leave."

He stared at me. I stared back until Dad sighed and gave in, pulling a chair out from the wall.

Catching waited until he was sitting by the bed. Then she rested her chin on her knees and started speaking, in a soft, contemplative tone that I hadn't heard from her before: "When I was in the beneath-place, it was stories that got me through. Stories that brought me home."

She tilted her head to one side, studying me and Dad. "But I don't know where the end of this story is going to take you two."

Outside, the wind began to gust, throwing dust into the air and blocking out the sunlight. As the room grew darker, the wind grew stronger, swirling past with a sound like rushing water. Weirdly, the sound seemed to be coming from all sides, as if the wind had somehow encircled the room and was blowing *inside* the hospital.

And Catching began: "People can time travel . . ."

Catching

THE TWO

People can time travel inside their heads.
Remember into the past.
Imagine into the future.
But sometimes you can't escape the now.

I'm being carried like a piece of meat.
First has my wrists.
Second has my ankles.
My head tips. My body's limp.
Can't run. Can't fight. Only endure. Like always.

They put me on the table. The one made of sticks.
They leave.
I'm not alone. Never alone.
There's breathing in the shadows.
Low, heavy breaths. The Feed.
Something about him is different.
I don't know what.

His palm presses against my stomach.
His fingers rip my flesh.
He digs for my soul.

It's harder for him to find colors.
He's taken so many.
He has to go deeper.
His hand brushes my spine. Grabs hold of a color. Yanks
it out.
A scream tears through my body.
No sound comes out of my mouth.
It's all locked inside.
With everything else.

The pain is too much.
My brain shuts down.
When it turns back on, I'm in my room.

I try to move my fingers.
They twitch. The drug's worn off.
My hand is all gray.
My arm too.
I'm turning into Crow.

"Why do you keep fighting?" she asks. "You should be a
dead girl!"
Makes sense.

If I'm dead inside, I'm free.

No.

If I'm dead inside, I'm *dead inside*.

I say the words:

"Granny . . ." *Trudy Catching.*

"Nanna . . ." *Sadie Catching.*

"Grandma . . ." *Leslie Catching.*

"Mum . . ." *Rhonda.*

"Me."

Crow joins in. But she adds new words now.

"Isobel's Granny. Crow's Granny."

"Isobel's Nanna. Crow's dad."

"Isobel's Grandma. Crow's friend."

"Isobel's mum. Crow's mum."

"Me. You. *Us.*"

Her people and mine carry me into sleep.

The door scrapes.

I wake.

Fetchers. Bread.

I eat.

But my arms drop to my sides.

My legs give way.

No! It's never twice so close together.

Then I realize what was different about the Feed.

His eyes weren't mirrors.

They were chips of brown stone.

There's not one Feed.

There's two.

THE DREAM

I've got no way to track time.
No sun.
No moon.
No ticking clocks.
Just the gray that eats my skin.
Have days gone by? Weeks? *Years?*

I'm on the bed.
Something splashes my pillow.
A tear.
Not mine. Crow's. She's hovering above me.

She's never cried for me before.

"Your color's almost all gone," she whispers. "When there's
no more, there's *no more.*"
I close my eyes.
Shut out the sight of my body.
"Say the words, Crow."

"Granny . . . Nanna . . . Grandma . . ."
We say words together until I fall asleep.

I'm walking on a hill.
The hill's green.
The sky's blue.
The wildflowers are red and yellow and orange and purple and
black.

Somebody's laughing.
I follow the sound.
Girls are sitting in a circle.
One looks at me. She has freckles on her nose.
"Are you here?" she asks. "We thought you were with Crow."
"You know Crow?"

They all laugh.
"Of course we do," says another. "She's fighting the wrong
fight."
"She's not!" I snap.
They speak together: "You can't fight feeling with not-feeling!"

I know who they are.
The girls who died.
"Am I dead?"
"Not yet," Freckles says. "But nearly."
I don't want to be dead.
Except . . .

These girls are happy. This place is pretty.
I'm not sure why I'm still fighting.

Wind tears across the hillside.
Slams into my chest.
Lifts me off my feet.
Spins me through the sky.

Freckles looks up as I fly over her.
"If you can name it, you can catch it," she calls. "If you
can catch it, you can fight it. Everything has its opposite.
Remember!"

The dream shatters.
Crow is screaming: "Isobel-the-Catching! Isobel-the-
Catching! Isobel-the-Catching!"
I sit up. Clap my hands over my ears. "Stop shouting!"
She stops.
My hands fall.
My arms weigh nothing.
Not dead yet. But nearly.
I'm slipping away.

Crow slams her hand against her head.
"I am stupid! You *refuse* to be a not-feeling dead girl. But
you were almost a real dead girl! Why did I wake you up?"
She slaps her head again. "Stupid Crow!"
She's been telling me from the start to be dead.

She just saved my life.
I giggle.
"*Not* funny!" she snaps.
But it is.

I laugh and laugh.
Crow stands under the light. Glares.
My laughter stops.
"Crow, your hair!"
"What about it? It is hair."
I point. My finger trembles. "It's *black*."
Not all black. But strands of darkness flow through the gray.
Crow finds one and holds it up. "My colors are gone. My
colors are *taken*."
My head spins. I lurch to my feet. "Colors can come back!"
I smile. She doesn't. She's scared.
"I do not *want* colors! I do not *want* to feel!"
She pulls at the black. Ripping it out. "Dead girl, gray girl,
dead girl, gray girl . . ."
"Crow, stop!"

I charge at her.
She dances away.
"You have done this, Isobel-the-Catching! *Words* have done
this. You have made me a not-gray girl!"
I lunge again. Crow's hand flashes down. Nails rake my
arm.
I yelp.

Crow lets go of her hair.

"I hurt you?" Her voice is small.

I inspect the cuts. Red blood leaks over my gray skin.

"It's not that bad."

"But I *cannot* hurt you. Cannot hurt, cannot touch, cannot feel . . ."

"You've got a color now! You're changing. Getting stronger."

She holds up both her hands.

Stares at them as if she's only just realized what hands can do.

What hands are for.

"Is there any color in *my* hair?" I ask.

"No. You are all gray."

Crow goes back to looking at her hands.

I slump on the bed.

Whatever's worked for her hasn't worked for me.

Everyone's gray is their own.

Maybe everybody's got their own way to get colors back.

I need to find mine.

If you can name it, you can catch it.

The girl in the dream said that. Freckles.

The sentence hammers my brain.

If you can name it, you can catch it.

If you can name it, you can catch it.

If you can name it . . .

Freckles could've meant the gray.
Except it's already got a name. It's the gray.
Another name?
You can't fight feeling with not-feeling.

I look down to my wrist.
The start of my gray.
I take a breath.
Close my eyes.
Remember that first time.

My stomach heaves.
My skin crawls.
But I know the name.
I open my eyes. Stare at my wrist. Say it.
"You are despair."

The gray gets lighter.
It makes the shape of long fingers.
This piece of gray is *caught*.

What I can catch, I can fight.
Everything has its opposite.
The opposite of despair?
Easy. Hope.
But I've got none.

That can't be right.
I've got to have some.

Colors can come back. That's hopeful.
But inside where hope should live, there's something smashed.
Something broken.

Despair rises.
The fingerprints sink back into the rest of the gray.
A tear slides down my cheek.
A name shines in my mind.
Granny Trudy Catching.
My Great-Great-Grandmother.

Mum's voice speaks:

Your old Granny was born into the frontier times, when white men first came to our homeland. Terrible things happened to her. There was nothing she could do about it. All her choices got taken away. But she drew strength from her homeland. Her family. Her people. She never forgot how to laugh. She never forgot how to love.

Your Granny knew how to hold on to who she was.

Connections light up across time and space.

Granny Trudy Catching.
Nanna Sadie Catching.
Grandma Leslie Catching.
Mum.
Me.

I find my way to myself.
To my strength.
I know who I am.
I know what I can do.
Hope flickers.
I stand.

The flicker grows into flames.
I walk to where the light glows from the ceiling.
Flames build to fire.
I hold my arm to the light.
Fire blazes out from my heart, up into my wrist.
There is a whooshing sound.
The mark of fingers disappears.

I stare at the part of me I've got back.
My soft skin.
The blue vein beneath.
The little freckle on the side.
It's beautiful. *I'm* beautiful.

Crow hops over.
Takes my wrist in a gentle grip.
"Not a dead girl."
She reaches up with her other hand, to pull her hair.
"Not a gray girl."
Finally: "No one comes?"

I get it. All this time, Crow believed three things:
The only way to stand your colors being taken is to be dead inside.
Once you're gray, you're gray forever.
No one's coming to stop the Feed.
Now she's asking . . .
What happens when the first two things are lies?

I tell her. "First, we catch the gray. Then we stop the Feed."

THE CATCHING

Crow's in her corner.
I can't see her.
Only hear her.
"You must become a dead girl. A not-feeling girl."
She giggles.
"We have no claws or wings or bite."
More giggling.
"No one gets away!"
She laughs so hard, she falls onto the floor.

Laughing off lies.
I wish I could get rid of my gray that way.
I can't. I've got to name.
Catch.
Fight.

My gray fights back.
But people can time travel inside their heads.
I catch a piece of gray: fear. And I remember.

The playground at school.
That bully, Billy King, stalking toward little Josie Lewis.
Me, stepping into his way.
Courage eats fear.
The Feed's handprint on my stomach disappears.

I move to the next stain on my skin.
This time, I go forward.
Crow and me on the beach.
She pushes me into the surf.
I grab hold of her. We tumble, laughing, into the waves.
Joy eats sadness.
Trails made by tears on my face and neck fade to nothing.

There's no way to know how long this is taking.
We've got no sun.
No moon.
No ticking clocks.
Just choices.
They measure the distance between who we are and who
we're turning into.
Except it's the same choice, made again and again.
Choose the opposite of gray.
It takes forever.
It takes a moment.

THE ESCAPE

Footsteps echo outside.
The door rattles.
Fetchers come in.
They stand. Loom.
They think they're bigger and stronger than us.

Not anymore.

Crow leaves her corner.
Her skin and eyes are brown.
Her hair and dress are black.
Her shadow on the wall is a thing of wing and claw and
bite.

Crow's hair sweeps across the ground to smash against the
Fetchers' ankles.
First gets knocked flat.
Second staggers. Crow darts in and slashes.
The top half of Second's mask falls off.
There's nothing beneath.

Second screeches and dives for his missing eyes.
I pounce on First's chest. Grip the edge of his mask.
He lurches up to his full height.
I hold on and swing, pulling with all my strength.
The mask comes free.
I fly across the room.
Hit the ground.
Roll.
Get to my feet with First's false face in my hand.

The empty space where his head should be screams.
"Give it back give it back give it back!"
I throw the mask against the wall.
It shatters.
First howls.

Heavy feet pound in the distance.
There's no more time for Fetchers.
"Crow! A Feed's coming!"
We charge out the door.
The Feed thuds down the tunnel.
His mirror eyes widen when he sees us.
He roars.
I turn to run away.

Crow grabs my arm. Spins me back around. "We stop the
Feed."
She's right. My mind knows it.
But my body wants to flee.

I haven't gotten rid of all my gray.

There's still a piece buried inside.

A gray that makes me want to hide from the Feed.

Choose the opposite of gray.

I face the Feed.

Straighten my shoulders.

Lift my head.

Stare into his eyes.

Name my last gray. "You're shame."

The Feed flinches. He thinks I'm naming him.

I *am* naming him.

"This gray's *yours*," I say. "My colors are *mine*. I'm not carrying your shame for what you did. Only my pride. For surviving you."

The last gray disappears.

Like it never existed.

It never should've.

Not inside me.

I'm not the one who should be running from him.

He should be running from me.

From *us*.

Crow sings:

"*No more for the Feed.*

No more in need.

Colors shine bright.

Today catchers fight.
Dead Feed, dead Feed . . . dead!"

The Feed runs.
We chase.
We follow the *thump, thump, thump* of footsteps.
The tunnels go everywhere and nowhere.

The *thump* stops.
He's run out of tunnel.
There's only a wall ahead.

The Feed punches the ceiling.
Blood drips down his arm.
He squeals in pain. Pulls himself up through the hole.
We tear after him, leaping up into . . .
The world.

The taste of fresh air in my mouth.
The feel of soft dirt under my feet.
The glow of the moon and stars above.
I stagger. Throw out my hand. Catch myself against a tree.
Crow tips back her head. Stretches out her arms like she
can hug the sky.
"We are rainbow girls, Isobel-the-Catching! We will bathe
in the clouds and sing in the sun, and let the world paint
our souls and our souls paint the world!"
"We will." I point. There's a light in the distance. "But not yet."

We go. We find a cage.
Light shines out from gaps between white wooden bars.
Birds of all colors huddle at the top.
The Feed stands at the bottom.
There's only one door.
It's shut. Locked.
The Feed smiles.
The birds call out: "Free us! Free us! Free us!"

Crow's hair rises to either side of her like wings.
Strands of black beat the air.
Wind gusts. The door rattles.
The Feed stops smiling.
The birds flutter in excitement.

Crow beats harder. The wind gets stronger.
The door rips from its hinges.
It spins into the night. Smashes into a tree.
Birds fly out in a rush, singing their thanks.
Tiny feathers float in the air.
We walk into the cage.

The Feed falls to his knees.
We circle him.
We're a loop that begins with me and ends with Crow.
Or begins with Crow and ends with me.
He cowers.
He changes.

His tall frame gets shorter.
His arms and legs shrink.
His eyes aren't mirrors.
He's lost his glasses in the chase.
The Feed is a man.

The man's head turns from side to side.
Tracking our movements.
His skin is sweaty. His lips tremble.
He's terrified. But it doesn't make me happy.
It doesn't make me anything.
Crow and I don't have to do this for ourselves.
Not anymore.
We have to do it because the Feed must be stopped.
Only we can stop him.
Only we *will*.

I put my face close to his. I can see into his brain.
"You'd like to think you're important to us. But you're not.
When this is done, all you'll be to us is a bad man we once
knew."
I step back.
"We won't think of you again."
Crow dances.
The world explodes.

Beth

THE END

As Catching's voice stopped, so did the wind.

The dust that had been swirling outside drifted down to the earth, letting the light back in. Except it was the soft light of morning instead of the bright light of the early afternoon.

"It's the next *day*?" I gasped. "How can it be the next day?"

Catching shrugged. "Like I said. Not a small ending."

She'd also said she didn't know where the end of her story would take us. I felt like it had carried me across an ocean to an unfamiliar land. Except I knew the world hadn't changed; the way I saw it had. Something fundamental had shifted in my head, and things were different now in ways I was struggling to define.

I glanced over at Dad and gasped again. He looked *bad*. His face was crumpled, not just around the edges the way it had been before, but all the way in. I hadn't seen him like this since right after I'd died. But he wasn't looking at me. He was looking at Catching.

"I'm sorry," he said to her. "I'm so sorry."

Her lip curled. "I told you. You're too late to save me."

"I know." His voice broke. My gaze flicked from him to her, puzzled. Then Catching said, "It's about a hundred paces to the west. We shut it up. Took the keys. But it'll be open for you."

"The keys to what?" I asked. "What's a hundred paces to the west?"

Neither of them answered me. Dad rose to his feet. *All* the way to his feet, drawing himself up to his full height in a way that made me realize he'd been slumping for months. His crumpled face smoothed out into hard, clear lines. I hadn't seen him like this since I was alive.

The lines in his face were deeper now, carved by pain, but otherwise he looked like the dad I'd known. Better, even—he looked like the man he would become, in a world where he lived even though I didn't. And I didn't know if Catching's story had taken him to a new place too, or if he'd been changing for a while, deep inside, or if it was a combination of both.

"Beth," Dad said, "it's time to go."

I hesitated, looking at Catching. But she didn't seem fragile the way she'd done after telling the earlier parts of her story. This ending had drained her, but it also seemed to have released something. There was a lightness about her that hadn't been there before.

Catching looked back at me and grinned. I blinked, not sure I was seeing right, but I was. An actual smile.

"Go on, Teller," she said. "I'll see you later. And don't worry so much. You'll know when you know."

My mind circled the end of Catching's story as I followed Dad out of the room, trying to puzzle out what it all meant. But as we emerged from the hospital, her last words suddenly seemed like excellent advice. I'd know when I knew, and in the meantime it was nice just to walk alongside Dad when he was so tall. I'd almost forgotten what it was like for him to be the teller and me the butterfly girl.

So I didn't ask any questions about where we were headed, or why, as we drove away. It was only when Dad called Allie to arrange for her to meet us that I learned we were going back to the beginning.

As we neared the children's home, though, Dad stopped the car.

"We can drive in further," I said, pointing to the stretch of narrow road ahead. "Heaps further."

"I know," Dad replied. "And I will. But I need to talk to you about something first."

There was a grimness in his voice that I didn't like. *I'm not worrying about things right now, Dad. You are.* "What is it?" I asked warily.

"There's going to be a point today when we get to a place, and when we get there, you can't come in. I need you to promise me that you won't."

He wanted me to stay away from something? I could do that. "Okay."

"This is important, Beth."

"I *said* okay." He continued to stare at me with worry in his face, until I added in a more serious voice, "Really, Dad. I won't."

He nodded, satisfied, and drove on to the home. Allie was already there, leaning against the side of her car and staring at the trees as she waited.

Dad parked and got out, walking over to Allie. "Did you bring what I asked for?"

She nodded, waving at two flashlights sitting on the hood of her car. Dad grabbed a flashlight and headed toward the ruins of the home. Allie took the other flashlight and followed after him.

"You really think there's something left out here to find?" she asked. "The whole area was already searched."

"Derek Bell was in charge of that search, yeah?"

"Um . . . yes. Does that matter?"

"Yes. I think it does."

Dad reached the edge of the ruins, swiveled, and began to walk away.

To the west.

In even strides.

Which he was counting under his breath.

Catching had meant one hundred paces from the *home*, and I didn't know how Dad had known that. But then, he'd been on the trail of an idea about this case since yesterday morning at Bell's place. And even thinking about what that idea might be made my head hurt again, like my brain was complaining about having to make connections too soon. I let my thoughts go and trailed after Dad and Allie, enjoying the walk through the cool morning air.

When Dad reached eighty paces, the wind came sweeping along the ground to gust past us, as if it was traveling ahead. *Crow? Like in the story?* I looked back, half expecting to see her, but there was no one there.

Dad kept going until he reached one hundred and stopped.

There was nothing here except trees and dirt.

"Did you get a tip or something?" Allie asked, in a tone that indicated that perhaps the tip hadn't been very reliable.

"Something like that," Dad replied. He didn't seem discouraged. Instead, he turned in a slow circle to survey his surroundings. After a second, he spotted something and took off at a run. Allie rushed after him and I rushed after her, the two of us tearing through the trees and into a big clearing.

There didn't seem to be anything here either. But Dad had stopped again and become fascinated with the ground. He was scanning the dirt, his gaze traveling back and forth across the space. Then he hurried forward into the shadow of an overhanging rock.

"Here!" he called.

I ran over and so did Allie. There was a metal door set into the ground, pushed back on its hinges to reveal a ladder going downward.

Allie gasped. "What is that?"

"You told me yourself that old Oscar Sholt thought the apocalypse was coming. I think he built a bunker."

Allie peered at something dark caked on the door. She paled. "Is that dried blood?"

"Looks like it to me."

"Hello?" she yelled. "Anyone down there?"

There was no answer. Allie shook her head. "Someone could be hurt." She clicked on her flashlight, tucked it under her chin, and began to descend the ladder.

Dad shot a stern look in my direction. I crossed the clearing to sit on a fallen log and called over to him, "See? Not going anywhere. I wouldn't break a promise to you, Dad."

He gave me an approving nod and climbed down the ladder after Allie, his feet echoing on the rungs as he disappeared into the earth below.

I rested my hands on the log and leaned back, listening to the rush of water from the river in the distance. The air was sharp with the tang of eucalyptus from the trees, and sunlight was filtering through the leaves to create patterns of light and shade on the ground. This seemed a pretty, peaceful place, and I was content to sit here for a while.

In the quiet, my mind felt as if it was relaxing into a new shape, adjusting to whatever shift had occurred within me as I'd been listening to Catching's story. Calm flowed from my brain through my body. For the first time since I'd died, I felt as if everything would be okay.

Then I noticed something glinting on the earth nearby, and went over for a better look.

It was a pair of glasses, half buried in the dirt.

Catching's story and my experiences in this town suddenly slammed together. Connections fired and popped through my mind. I yelped in pain, clutching my hands to my head as everything meshed into one sequence of events.

Then it was over, and I let my hands fall, looking around the clearing with new eyes.

The fallen log I'd been sitting on was at one side of the clearing.

On the other, the overhanging rock Dad had ducked under resembled an egg lying on its side.

There were mirror eyes in the dirt at my feet.

This clearing was where the Fetchers had taken Isobel Catching. The tunnels were the bunker. The cage of birds with its white wooden bars was the weatherboard children's home. And I'd seen these gold-rimmed glasses before—in the photograph Dad had shown me when we'd first come to the home.

One of the Feeds was Alexander Sholt.

His *was* the body found after the fire.

And I knew who'd killed him. I knew who'd killed them all.

Sounds came from the bunker. Someone was climbing the ladder, and they were doing it fast. Allie came bolting out and dashed into the trees to double over and throw up.

Steadier footsteps followed hers, and Dad came out too. He didn't vomit. But he looked like he wanted to. He walked to the rock and put both hands against it, leaning into the stone and ducking his head to take one deep breath after another.

After a few more minutes of retching, Allie ran out of food to bring up. She straightened, wiping the back of her arm across her face, and called in a shaky voice, "I'm going to the river. To wash out my mouth."

Dad waved his hand in acknowledgment but kept leaning into the rock. I walked over to him, but I didn't speak. He didn't seem capable of talking right now.

Eventually Allie returned, weaving through the trees and back into the clearing. She was dead white and seemed to have aged ten years.

Dad straightened as she approached. The two of them exchanged a long, worn-out look, as if they were carrying the weight of the world between them.

Allie spoke first: "People were held in there."

"Girls," Dad said. "More than one."

She gave a jerky nod. "There was a jacket. On a table. I don't know if you saw—"

"I saw."

"Of course you did." She hugged her arms around herself. "The thing is, I *know* that jacket. It's Derek Bell's. I've seen him wear it a thousand times. This . . . this is what he was involved in, isn't it?"

The second Feed.

And I'd met him.

Talked to him.

Not known what he was.

Catching had once told Dad he'd say there was no such thing as monsters. There were. But me and the rest of the world had only seen the men.

"I think he was a part of it, yes," Dad said to Allie. "Along with Alexander Sholt. And Cavanagh and Flint, who were both being paid off. For their silence, I assume. And their cooperation. Some of the victims could have been from the home."

She made a gasping sound, as if someone had struck her chest. "How could they be a part of this? How could anyone? And for *money*?"

"Not just money. Power. Importance. The kind of sick delight people like that get out of things like this. I never did meet Cavanagh or Flint." His gaze flicked to me, then away. "But they strike me as people with no moral core."

No heart, no guts, no core. Here, they serve the Feed.

Allie's eyes widened. "We need to put a warrant out for Alex Sholt! He could be—"

Dad held up a hand. "First, I asked my boss yesterday to get people onto Sholt. But second, I'm certain we're going to find that the body from the fire at the home *is* Alexander Sholt."

She blinked, absorbing that. Dad drew in a deep breath, as if he was preparing himself for something, and I knew what it would be. He was looking at Allie with such compassion that it was obvious what news he was about to break. I wished he didn't have to tell her. I figured he probably wished that too, every time he had to tell a family that someone wasn't coming back. I didn't know how he could bear it.

He gave her one piece of information at a time, trying to lead her to it: "I think Derek Bell and Alexander Sholt started down this path a very long time ago. Back when they were teenagers. We're going to have to bring in dogs to search this area for bodies, and we'll find more than one. I think we'll even find the first one."

She nodded, like that made sense. She didn't understand. Not until Dad added gently, "And I think the first one was buried around twenty years ago."

Shock rippled across her face. *"No."*

He sighed. "Allie—"

She took a step back, holding up a hand like she could ward off his words. "Sarah's not dead. She's *alive.* She's alive, and she's out there somewhere, and I'm going to find her!"

"I'm sorry," Dad said quietly. "We are going to find her. But not alive."

Her hand dropped. She staggered to the fallen log and sat. Dad went over to sit beside her. Dad was still tall, but Allie had become little and was growing littler by the second.

When she spoke, even her voice was tiny: "We need to get police out here. To process all this. And it has to be the ones from the city." Her lips curved into a bitter snarl. "Not me, or any other cop too dumb to see what their boss really was."

"You—"

But she rounded on him. "Don't even try to tell me this isn't my fault. I should have known. I was her best friend. And I'm a *police officer.*"

"Then *be* a police officer!" he snapped back.

Her mouth fell open in surprise.

Dad waved at the bunker. "You think this is the end of the investigation? It's just the beginning. Did children go missing from that home? And how many people, whose job it was to check on the welfare of kids, *failed to notice* something was wrong here? Who else around here did know? I can tell you now, I think Derek's father covered for his son. I'll bet Alexander Sholt's father knew something too, even if it wasn't all of it."

Allie closed her mouth, an arrested expression on her face. "That was why Gerry Bell didn't investigate properly? It was on *purpose*? How about the deaths of Flint and Cavanagh— do you think Derek had something to do with that? But . . . he was killed too."

"He was, and probably with the same weapon," Dad said. "Sholt died first. So maybe there was a falling-out between Sholt and Derek, and Derek kills him. The fire's just faulty wiring, bad luck—but it throws everything into chaos.

"After that, I think it could have gone something like this: Derek convinces Charles Sholt to say nothing about his son being missing. Maybe he tells him Alexander is on the run; maybe he tells him the truth about Alexander being dead but throws the blame on someone else. He convinces the old man to keep quiet for the sake of the family name and to give Derek a chance to cover things up.

"Then Derek has to get rid of the director and the nurse, presumably because they know what he's done and he doesn't have the cash to pay them off—the money they've gotten in the past all came from Alexander Sholt. So they die next. But now . . ."

Dad shook his head. "Now old man Sholt is getting

suspicious about what happened to his son and has the resources to hire someone to do something about it. You saw those windows at Derek's house; he was trying to protect himself from someone. And if this *is* how it all went down, then having Derek killed with the same weapon—which Derek probably had somewhere in that house—might have been Charles Sholt's idea of an artistic touch."

Wow. For a complete fabrication, I thought that was really quite convincing. Allie was certainly buying it. She'd been nodding along with Dad's words, and I could see that he was pleased with her reaction. He was testing out the story, I realized, to see if people would believe it.

Because he absolutely couldn't tell anybody the truth.

"It might have gone differently, of course," Dad said. "We'll probably never know all the details. But one way or another, there's going to be a lot to do to make sure justice is finally done for every girl Bell and Sholt hurt. If you're not up for that, you'd better tell me now."

Allie lifted her chin. "I'm up for it."

I was relieved to hear that her voice had expanded back to its normal size. In fact, all of her seemed to be expanding. She was still reeling from this, and would be for a while, but she'd be okay for as long as she had something to do. For as long as there was justice to be done. And I guessed there always would be justice to be done for somebody somewhere. So Allie would be okay.

Dad gave a brisk nod. "Good. I'm going to start making calls. But my colleagues from the city aren't going to be able to find their way out here from the home unescorted. Do you think you could go back there and wait for them?"

"Of course." She rose to her feet, shoulders squared, and went marching through the trees like a soldier with a mission.

The wind chased after her, swirling leaves into her path and ruffling her hair. For a second, Allie stopped, looking upward to a sky that would be littered with stars come nightfall. The turmoil inside her seemed to lighten a little. Then she kept walking.

Dad stayed quiet until she'd vanished from sight. Then he asked, "Do you understand now, Beth?"

"Yeah."

But I could see from his expression that he thought I was missing something. Then he did something terrible. He looked at me with the same compassion he'd shown to Allie.

"Beth," Dad said slowly, "Isobel Catching didn't survive."

That made no sense. "What? No—she escaped, the night of the fire—"

But he was shaking his head. "She died, Beth. The night of the fire, or before that."

"That's impossible! She's the witness. She's in the hospital—how can she be dead?"

"Do you remember what happened at the hospital, right before we met Catching?"

I did remember. I'd looked through a door into a room, and seen a dark-haired girl. Then Catching had called out to Dad and— *Oh.*

"You think that *other* girl was the witness?"

He nodded. "She's the girl who ran away from rehab. Catching came here exactly as she said, on a road trip with her mum. A few months ago, because that was when the storm hit, the big one that caused all that property damage. No one was reported as dead, but that's not because no one died. No one was *found,* probably because Derek Bell covered up the accident. Catching wandered away from the wreck—wounded and disorientated—ended up near the home, and was discovered by the director and the nurse."

"But you can see her! You've been talking to her all this time."

"Yeah." He rose to his feet. "Just the way I talk to you, Beth."

He thought I wasn't the only ghost he could see. What Dad was saying made sense. So why was I still so certain that Catching wasn't dead?

It was something to do with the story. Something in it told me she'd made it out alive . . . only I wasn't sure what. Before I could think it through, Dad spoke again: "I thought I could help her. But we didn't get here at the beginning. We got here when it was all over. We got here at the end."

He was right that we'd arrived after the fire, the night the world exploded. But he was wrong about it being all over . . . for a reason I couldn't quite articulate.

Then a voice from behind us said it for me. "*Of course* you're here at the end. So what? It's the beginning that hasn't happened yet."

THE BEGINNING

I swung around to face Catching. She wasn't wearing the hospital gown anymore. Instead, her long jumper had grown longer, flowing around her arms and legs to clothe her in green brightness. There was a glossy black bird perched upon her left shoulder. Crow. *Sarah.*

Living people couldn't pop into existence like this. My heart sank.

"You're dead?" I whispered.

She shrugged. "Just appeared out of nowhere, didn't I?"

But that wasn't a yes. It was a Catching evasion, one of her answers that wasn't really an answer.

I'm not wrong. I'm not. I began to run through the story in my head, trying to figure out what had truly happened to her. But Catching wasn't finished speaking to me yet: "Do you understand what the story was for now?"

To be heard. Except I wasn't sure even Catching knew everything she'd been trying to say. But I knew what she'd wanted *me* to hear. And I knew she'd never been telling the story to Dad. "You told the story to show me how to move on."

185

Catching waved in the direction of the home. "Crow saw you there, the day you came. She thought you might be trapped. So I put myself in your way, to find out why you were still on this side of the world."

Crow tilted her head to one side, fixing a bright, hopeful eye upon me, like she was asking if I remembered her.

The crow on the rubble. The one that I'd waved at, not truly believing it could see me. "I remember."

She preened and flapped off to land on a branch of a nearby tree. Dad tracked her path through the air with a faint smile on his lips; I could tell he was pleased to see Sarah Blue flying free.

Then he turned to Catching and said, "I promise you I will make sure Gerry Bell and Charles Sholt, and anyone else who was involved in any way and is still alive, is held to account. But you have to leave this to the police from now on."

Why was he ignoring Crow? Catching's glance met mine, and I saw the laughter in it. That was when I realized: Dad didn't know.

"Um, Dad? It wasn't her."

Dad gave an impatient shake of his head. "She's different to you, Beth—she can affect things in this world, Beth. I'm sure of it."

"It's not that," I told him. "You've missed all the clues. Flint and Cavanagh were dragged out of Sholt's second-story window and dropped into that drain from above. That was why the window was smashed, and why there was no broken lock on the fence. The fire screen in Derek's house was knocked over because something came down the chimney. And the blade with the curve? It wasn't a knife. It's a *beak*."

Dad's mouth fell open. Then his gaze went to where Crow was sitting with her shadow stretching out behind her. A thing of claw and wing and bite.

He let out a startled exclamation and took a hasty step back.

Crow threw back her head and cackled.

Dad kept staring, his gaze flicking between the shadow on the ground and the bird in the tree as if he couldn't quite comprehend what he was seeing.

"She's lots of things at once, Dad," I said. "Little, and *really* big. Old and young. A girl and a bird. She's . . . Crow."

After a second, Dad stepped forward again and called up at Crow: "I know you were failed by the police. I'm so sorry for that. More sorry than you can know. But you can trust me to do this, and you can trust Allie. You've stopped the Feeds. You've stopped the Fetchers. Let us deal with the rest."

Crow stared down at him for a long moment. Then she bobbed her head in agreement. Dad's shoulders sagged in relief and he pulled out his phone, striding away to make the call.

I looked up at Crow. How many times had I seen crows around town and never noticed that one was just a bit bigger and a bit glossier than all the others? How often had there been mysterious gusts of wind at exactly the right moment? Crow had been there all along, trying to impart to me the gift of her hard-won knowledge— *Wait.*

Something about that thought had triggered a connection in the part of my mind that was still puzzling over the story. What was it? But I knew. Gifts. *Strengths!* Everything came together, and I finally knew what had happened to Isobel Catching.

I glared at her indignantly. "You're not dead."

Something sparked in her eyes. "You reckon not?"

"I *know* not. It's all in the story. At the end, before you escaped, you found your way back to your self. You found your *strength*. That's what gave you the hope you needed to start fighting the gray. You knew you could get out, because you knew what you could do."

She didn't say anything. But I was sure I was on the right path. "Except your strength must have been growing in you before then. It had already helped Crow. That was why she could scratch your arm, when she'd never been able to affect anything before. It was why I could only make a light explode *after* I met you. Because you touch different sides of the world at once, and it makes you a kind of . . . conduit."

Catching watched me. Waiting for me to come out and say it. So I did. "*I* think the story of the gifts of the Catching women goes like this: Your Granny could hold on to her self, and your Nanna could swim like a fish, and your Grandma knew how to endure, and your mum could see people who'd passed over. But you?" I shook my head, still a little astonished by it. "You can *walk all the sides of the world.*"

She grinned. The second actual smile I'd got from her today.

"How do you do it?" I demanded.

"Dunno. How did you do it? You almost got to another side once. The one with the colors."

For a second, I wondered how she knew that; then I realized Crow must have told her. It had been Crow who'd been chasing me, after all.

"That was different! I'm dead; I'm kind of supposed to be on that side. I'm not even properly here."

She shrugged. "I'm properly everywhere. It's all the same world."

Which I guessed made sense if you could see all the sides the way she must be able to.

"You coming with me, Teller?" Catching asked. "Crow is."

"Coming where?"

"I'm going to the colors. My mum's there. I want to see her. After that?" She shrugged. "Maybe I'll stay in the colors forever. Maybe I won't. I'll decide when I decide."

From above, Crow made a plaintive noise, shifting from one foot to the other in an anxious dance.

"It's all right," Catching told her. "Wherever we go, we'll go together." Then to me, "You coming or not?"

No. I have to take care of my father. But those words didn't feel true anymore. Instead, I said, "I have to talk to my father."

Who at that moment was in the middle of what looked like a super-intense conversation with his boss as he gave her the details of what had been going on in this town.

"Um. Just not right now."

"S'alright," Catching said. "We'll wait."

She strolled over to sit on the fallen log. I sat with her, and Crow flapped to a perch in a tree above us. The three of us watched as the clearing filled with police officers.

Dad was on and off his phone, talking to the city. Allie hung around the fringes, wanting to be available in case any local knowledge was needed, but not wanting to put herself in the midst of the investigation into her dead boss.

The morning grew warmer and the light brighter as the sun rose higher. And eventually there came a moment when I looked over at Dad, only to find he was looking at me.

It was time.

I rose and walked away from the clearing, waving to him to follow. I kept going until we were well into the trees, where no one would hear Dad talking. Then I turned to face him. Only I wasn't quite sure how to begin this conversation.

He began it for me. "You're leaving, aren't you?"

Well, yes, I probably was, but I'd been planning to gently build up to that. "Um. Yeah. Catching and Crow are going to the colors. I thought I might go with them."

"But you're worried about me."

"Hey, stop saying my thoughts before I do! How do you even know them?"

His eyes crinkled in amusement. "I know because I'm your dad. And I realize I haven't been acting like it for a while. I'm sorry, Beth. It got so I didn't know how to go on living. I didn't even think I *should* go on, without you."

"That's upside-down thinking, Dad!"

"I know. I can see now that what I've been doing . . ." He shook his head, his eyes darkening with anger at himself. "It's no way to honor who you were. Who you *are*. And I want to be someone you can look up to, Beth. I want to go on being your dad, even though . . ."

His voice broke. He sucked in a deep breath and continued. "Even though you won't be here. I want you to know, wherever you are, that I'm a dad you can be proud of."

There were tears running down his cheeks; down mine too. I knew I couldn't stay, but that didn't make it easy to go. This was hard, and awful, and it was making my heart twist in my chest. And I wanted something. I wanted it more than I'd ever wanted anything, ever. If strong emotions and Catching's presence were the key to spirits being able to touch this side, then I had both.

I flung my arms around my father. And I was *solid*. He gave a surprised grunt and hugged me back. We clung on to each other for a few last, precious moments. Then I felt my solidity fading, and I let him go.

His face was crumpled again. But only around the edges. There was strength in the middle.

"I love you, Dad. I'll always be your daughter."

"I love you, Bethie. I'll always be your dad."

He turned away from me in a slow, jerky movement. Then he began walking, putting one determined foot in front of the other. As he went, he pulled out his phone and made a call.

"Viv? It's Michael. Listen, I was just calling about Grandpa Jim's birthday—did you want me to bring anything to the party? Besides a present, I mean. Of course I'm coming! It'll be good to see you."

Aunty Viv was talking loud and fast, like she was trying to cram months' worth of missed conversations into one phone call. I had no idea what she was saying, and I wasn't sure she was making much sense. But it didn't matter. What mattered was Dad was speaking to her again.

What mattered was that he was showing me he was choosing the opposite of gray.

I kept watching until he'd disappeared through the trees. The second he'd vanished from sight, a voice said, "Ready, Beth-the-Teller?"

I spun around to face a girl with brown skin and brown eyes and black hair that flowed like a cloak.

Catching was standing beside her. She raised an eyebrow, and I realized she was waiting for an answer to Crow's question.

"I'm ready," I said.

Crow held out her hand to me, and I took it. She used her other hand to grab hold of Catching's and shouted, "Let's run!"

So we ran, me in my yellow dress and Catching in green and Crow in black, three colors weaving through the trees. We ran as you could only run when you weren't alive or when you could walk between all the sides of the world. We ran without limits, getting faster and faster until we were flying with our feet on the ground.

Then Crow let go of us and launched herself into the

air. Her body seemed to dissolve into color, becoming every shade of black I'd ever seen, and a thousand more that I'd never known existed, swirling away into the sky above.

Catching threw back her head and laughed the first laugh I'd ever heard from her, a musical, husky sound that seemed to fill the forest. Then she leaped after Crow and became green, rising up to mingle with Crow's black.

My turn. I went spinning into a leap and melted into yellow, becoming the love I had for my dad, my Grandpa, my Aunties and my Uncles and the cousins, and for Catching and for Crow.

Other colors came to whirl around us, shouting their joy in our presence and welcoming us home.

We found my mum and Catching's mum, and Crow's family too. We bathed in the clouds and sang in the sun and let the world paint our souls and our souls paint the world.

And wherever we went, we went together.

AUTHORS' NOTE

We are Aboriginal storytellers. Our perspective is shaped by the culture and history of the Palyku people, from whom we come; our individual knowledge and experiences; and the collective inheritance of our Ancestors. But we are two voices amongst the many Aboriginal peoples and nations of Australia, and we speak for ourselves alone; there is not a single Aboriginal story, nor a definitive Aboriginal experience.

In telling this tale, we were informed by two sets of stories that are the inheritance of Aboriginal peoples. The first set is stories of our homelands, families, cultures—the stories that speak to the connections that sustain us and that we sustain in turn. The second set is the tales that entered our worlds with colonization—stories of the violence that was terrifyingly chaotic or, even more terrifyingly, organized on a systemic scale. Both sets of stories inform our existences and, thus, our storytelling.

The ancient tales of Aboriginal nations of Australia tell of an animate world, where everything lives. This includes not only animals, plants, and humans but also rocks, wind, rain, sun, moon. And so Aboriginal family connections extend beyond human beings to encompass all life. These connections can also reach past one cycle of existence to shape the next. For example, a person with a particular connection to dingoes may have been a dingo before, and will be one again. So it is with Crow. As Beth says at the end of the book, Crow is "lots of things at once . . . little, and *really* big. Old and young. A girl and a bird. She's . . . Crow."

Aboriginal stories also tell of a nonlinear world, one in which time does not run in a line from the past through the present and on into the future. All life is in constant motion, turning and rotating in relation to other life, and it is through these movements that the world shifts forward or back. In the words of Beth's Grandpa Jim: "Life doesn't move through time . . . Time moves through life." So the extent to which an event is "past" is not measured by the passage of years but rather by the degree to which affected relationships have been brought into balance. Thus, the journeys of Catching, Beth, Crow, and Michael do not "advance" because days pass by, but because these characters are finding ways to heal. Each of them ultimately reaches a point of transformation where they move out of one cycle and into another. This is why Catching says to Michael, at the conclusion of the book: "It's the beginning that hasn't happened yet."

One way to heal is through storytelling. As Catching knows, it is stories that get you through and bring you home. And many Aboriginal stories tell of the multigenerational trauma of colonialism, including the terrible pain inscribed onto the hearts and minds and bodies of Indigenous women. For Catching's family, this includes the heartbreak of the Stolen Generations.

For around one hundred years, beginning in the latter half of the nineteenth century, Indigenous children were taken from their families under laws and policies of successive Australian governments. The Australian Human Rights Commission has estimated that between one in three and one in ten Indigenous children were forcibly removed between 1910 and 1970, and that no Indigenous family escaped the effects of this removal. (Interested readers can find a copy of the report and other resources, including testimonies from Stolen Generations members, at bth.humanrights.gov.au.) For many families, including our own, more than one generation of children was taken away. This leaves Aboriginal families with the dual legacy of terrible heartbreak and the strength it took to survive. And it is by drawing on the resilience of her Ancestors that Catching is able to survive when her own life is threatened.

The final step in Catching's path to her own strength is shown to her by the experiences of her Great-Great-Grandmother, a woman who lived through the hard days of the frontier and was robbed of all her choices. But Catching's old Granny knew how to hold on to her self—with laughter, with love, and through her connections to her family and her homeland.

Catching, Beth, and Crow all ultimately find their way to themselves and raise their voices to defy all that would diminish them, including the things they have internalized.

And so the story begins, ends, and begins again with what always lay at the core of this tale: the enduring strength of Aboriginal women and girls.

197

ABOUT THE AUTHORS

Ambelin and Ezekiel Kwaymullina are a brother-sister team of Aboriginal writers who come from the Palyku people of the Pilbara region of Western Australia. They've worked together on a number of short novels and picture books. *The Things She's Seen* is their first joint young adult novel. They believe in the power of storytelling to create a more just world.